THE SHOTS FROM MARS

We have reason to believe that the Martians have now been warned about the Earth/Annwn bacteria and will come prepared to deal with it. Conclusive evidence of the coming invasion will soon be visible to your astronomers. Your scientists will have the advantage of having read the history of our invasion, an excellent work called *The War of the Worlds* by Mr. H. G. Wells. Your military men will be able to figure out how best to counteract the devastating power of the would-be conquerors.

However you will be handicapped by the existence of a group, originating on Earth, which holds that the Martians are superior beings to men and as such deserve to survive more than mankind does. One of its members is not only a brilliant scientist but is also a veritable Napoleon of crime as well.

As soon as it was ascertained that the leadership of this cult had crossed into Annwn through the Shimmering Gates, I was dispatched to this planet myself to spread the word of alarm. The question is: is it already too late? For now the Martians with their heat rays and their tripods have found allies —among their intended victims!

THE SECOND WAR OF THE WORLDS

George H. Smith

DAW BOOKS, INC.

DONALD A. WOLLHEIM, PUBLISHER

1301 Avenue of the Americas
New York, N. Y.   10019

FIRST PRINTING, OCTOBER 1976

1 2 3 4 5 6 7 8 9

PRINTED IN U.S.A.

In the last years of the nineteenth century after the founding of the city, no one would have believed that Annwn was being keenly and closely watched by an intelligence greater than man's, yet as mortal as his own; that as men busied themselves about their various concerns, they were being scrutinized and studied almost as narrowly as a man with a microscope might examine the transient creatures that swarm and multiply in a drop of water. With infinite complacency, men traveled to and fro over the globe tending to their little affairs, serene in their assurance of their empire over matter. It is possible the infusorians under the microscope do the same. No one gave a thought to the older worlds of space as sources of human danger; the idea of life upon them was generally dismissed as impossible or improbable.

Chapter 1

The fog that seemed to drift in directly off the Ice Sea at dusk was so thick it both muffled and exaggerated sound. Air horns of steamers on the wide estuary called the Silver Strand sounded as though they were on the street just below the windows of Dylan MacBride's cozy bachelor digs at 12 Fishmonger Row, but the heavy thump of a drayer's wagon and the *clop, clop, clop* of iron-shod horses' hooves on cobblestones directly under the windows sounded faint and muffled.

Dylan had dined early at the Army-Navy Club with Commander Noel Bran ap Lynn, his comrade in arms during the recent Goggish War. Anticipating the return of the fog that had plagued the city of Avallon for a week, Dylan had hurried home immediately after dinner, passing up a game of billiards with his friend. Now he was intently bending over charts spread out on a large oak table in one corner of his sitting room, listening to the wood fire crackling and spitting and wondering if a coal fire wouldn't have been better. Somehow a wood fire with its cheerful sounds and fragrant smells seemed more suitable for this chill night in early autumn.

The charts over which he labored with scale and mapping pen were of the waters surrounding the south polar regions of Annwn, where the famous Ice Caves were located on the sprawling, almost continent-sized island of Issapon. For the past three years, Dylan, an explorer whose father had been an explorer before him, had had it in mind to lead an expedition to those mysterious caverns. He wished to test out the theories of certain natural philosophers that the caves were the entry to even larger caverns beneath the earth and perhaps to the hollow center of Annwn itself. The Goggish War and the period of reconstruction that followed had interrupted his plans; then a somewhat stormy courtship of the beautiful redheaded priestess of Keridwen, Clarinda MacTague, had kept him from the task. But now he was well into the planning of the expedition and was correcting the charts he would need by making changes as indictated in the most recent *Notice To Mariners* issued by the Hydrographic Office. His preparations had taken a spurt forward because of the recent grant he had received from Caer Arinhood, the great Midlands university, to finance the proposed exploration.

It would be good to get into the field again, Dylan was thinking, to captain a stout ship on far seas and see sights that none had seen before him. He made further corrections in the sounding markings for the approach to the Crystal Lagoon. The mouths of the caves were located there on white sandy beaches, free of ice the year round because of subterranean volcanic action.

He had just lettered in *mean high water approach channel to Crystal Lagoon 7.3 ft.*, indicating that a vessel of any draft would have a better chance of entering the channel at high tide. Yes, it would be good to get back to the sea and—

The loud rattle of the wirephone interrupted his work and he laid the pen down carefully, wishing that electromatic communications had never been invented.

"Sure, now, and I know what you've been thinkin'!" The thick brogue on the other end of the line was unmistakable. "You think it'll be good to be gettin' out from under me eye and you needn't deny it!"

"Clarinda, I was thinking no such thing!" He stopped and stared at the speaking tube in consternation. There were no wires in Trogtown, so how could . . .

"Aw, 'tis nothin'. I just reached out with me mind and rattled the wire in your head," Clarinda said. "Keridwen lets me do things like that from time to time."

Dylan slammed down the speaking tube and flipped off the switch, but the girl's voice was still in his mind.

Now don't be gettin' miffed with your ladylove, Dylan, me darlin'. I was just sittin' here rockin' the wee one when I thought what a nice thing it would be to be talkin' to you and—

"Clarinda, I told you, I'm busy tonight," Dylan said out loud. This thing that Clarinda called mind speaking was most disconcerting. He loved her madly, but her ability to enter his mind at will was a power he found hard to bear.

And so you are, busy makin' little letterin's on a chart of a place that's so far away I won't even be able to touch you with me mind. He could almost see the full red lips pouting. *Is that what you be wantin'?*

"No, of course not, but . . . I guess you really wouldn't be able to read my mind at that distance, would you?"

Oh, so it's readin' your mind that's worryin' you! Well, it's an uninterestin' story and I'll just be puttin' down the book! There was a rude click as she turned him off and left him standing staring at the wall.

Before he could go back to his charts the wire rattled again. Thinking that Clarinda had changed her mind, he thought the words at her, *Oh, so you've come back, have you?*

There was no response, not even the faint sensation of warmth her thoughts caused in his mind. The wire rattled again. Convinced that it was another of Clarinda's tricks, he reluctantly reached for the speaking tube.

But it was a strongly accented man's voice which said in his ear, "Do I have the extreme honor, sir, of addressing Mr. Dylan MacBride, the explorer?"

"I am Dylan MacBride, yes."

"And I, sir, am Professor Bartolome Lombosa. It is that you have heard of me, no?"

"No, I'm afraid not," Dylan said.

"But I am known to all as the famous inventor of the electromatic gyroscopic car and the nonlethal poison dart gun. And now I have outdone myself with the greatest invention of all, my diving ram."

"Nonlethal poison dart gun?" Dylan said. "That might be useful on an exploration trip."

"Unfortunately, it is not completely developed yet," the professor said. "The poison has a tendency to lose its effectiveness while moving through the air, and for some reason I haven't worked out yet, the needle of the dart won't penetrate skin."

"Well, that does make it nonlethal," Dylan said.

"Yes, yes, indeed. That part of the experiment is a complete success."

"Well, tell me about the electromatic gyroscopic car," Dylan said, wondering why the man had called him. "I don't recall seeing anything like that on the streets."

"Technical and monetary difficulties," the professor said. "It is that the gyroscope does not hold the single-wheeled vehicle upright. The makers of motor carriages are blind to its possibilities and will not invest money in its development, even as the government is blind to the possibilities of my diving ram as a weapon of war and will not finance new engines for it. I am therefore giving this wonderful opportunity to you, sir!"

"Wonderful opportunity?" Dylan said, puzzled. "I don't understand what you're talking about."

"It is that I am offering you the unprecedented chance to help yourself by financing the development of the diving ram."

"But I'm not in the business of weapons of war," Dylan protested. "As you mentioned yourself, I am an explorer."

"Then it is the diving ram you need to explore, is it not?" Lombosa insisted. "The Ice Caves you can go into with the ram. It will cut the ice and dive under it most efficiently as soon as a few details of technical difficulty are solved."

The professor's dart gun that wasn't powerful enough to penetrate skin and his gyroscopic car that wouldn't stay upright weren't much recommendation for his diving ram, Dylan thought, but he had to concede the concept had possibilities. He had been negotiating for an old steam schooner, the *Pole Star*, that his father had used in Basham expeditions, but this was something new to think about.

"Exactly what are these technical difficulties?" he asked.

"Details . . . mere details," the professor said quickly.

"What kind of details?"

"The engines," the professor said. "They are not powerful enough perhaps. The speed is limited to less than three knots, and there is the matter of the freeboard."

"Freeboard?"

"The craft has just a little tendency to submerge," Lombosa said.

"I understood that was its function," Dylan said.

"To submerge when it is expected to submerge or—what is the word?—to float perhaps," the professor said. "This is an embarrassment when the hatches are open to provide air for the crew."

Dylan thought of the mountainous seas often encountered in the waters of the polar regions. "It sounds about as seaworthy as a railroad locomotive," he said.

"Oh, I would say somewhat more so, but perhaps not so fast," the professor said cheerfully.

"And the military has turned down this wonder ship?"

"Blind! Always blind to innovation," Lombosa said. "Admirals and generals can never see beyond their epaulets."

"I can't imagine why they would overlook the possibilities of a craft capable of three knots at full power that has a tendency to sink when it should float," Dylan said. "It would make a fearsome weapon of war . . . to those on board."

"It is perhaps that you make fun?" Lombosa sounded bewildered.

"It is possible," Dylan admitted. "But really, Professor Lombosa, your craft is hardly suitable for my needs. I require a strong, seaworthy vessel which can carry a heavy load of supplies, stand up to heavy seas, resist the pressure of ice and—"

"And dive under and cut its way through the ice, is it not so?"

"Those qualities would be helpful, but without the others, I don't see what value they would have," Dylan said.

The professor wasn't to be turned off so easily. "I will demonstrate the terrible diving ram *Thunderbolt* at eight of time tomorrow in the morning," he announced. "If Mr. Dylan MacBride would be present, his eyes will be astonished."

Maybe it wouldn't hurt to have a look, Dylan thought. If the craft had any possibilities at all, he really should investigate and, after all, what did he have to lose?

"The gentleman would have the opportunity to inspect and take voyage in *Thunderbolt* and to learn how much it will cost to charter it with a fixing of engines."

That was what he had to lose: money invested in engines for a vessel that wasn't seaworthy to start with. But still, it wouldn't hurt to take a look.

"Where is the *Thunderbolt* tied up?" Dylan asked.

"At the old Volksrend Steamship Company docks ten miles south of the city on the Silver Strand. Do you know the way?"

Dylan knew the place. During the Goggish investment of the city, the old docks had been the last facility still open for supplies and reinforcements from the south. It was a pleasant ride out along the tow paths on the embankment between the Strand and the Great South Canal. If he invited Clarinda, it would be a pleasant outing for both of them. Perhaps she could pack a picnic lunch. No, it might be better to have the Jepson caterers on High Street pack the lunch. Clarinda had some peculiar Hibernian idea of what constituted edible food, including a soup that looked and smelled like the water she washed the clothes of her numerous little brothers and sisters in.

"Yes, Professor, I know the way. I will be there at eight sharp with a lady friend."

"Ah, a lady friend," Lombosa said. "Perhaps a rich lady friend?"

"Rich only in beauty." Dylan laughed. "She is a priestess of Keridwen."

"A goddess of war, is it, of the Sassenach?"

"Of love and of the Cymru," Dylan said.

"Then perhaps she could cast a spell that would bring a

love of ironclad diving rams to the Board of Admiralty."

"I don't think so," Dylan said. "Keridwen is a pacifist."

"And so it would seem," the professor said, "is the Board of Admiralty."

If he was to have the pleasure of Clarinda's company for a canter beside the Strand in the morning, Dylan had to get in touch with her, and there were no wires connecting the upper city with Trogtown, the ancient city below the streets.

Dylan had no idea how to project his thoughts but it seemed worth a try. "Clarinda? Clarinda, are you there, sweetheart? Dylan calling Clarinda. Dylan calling Clarinda. Keridwen, if you're listening, great lady, would you care to relay my message?"

No answer. None of the warm fluttering feeling in his mind that meant the redheaded priestess was present.

The wire rattled again and he picked it up.

"Keridwen isn't available for messenger service!" Clarinda said tartly.

"Clarinda, it's you I want to talk to. I was trying to contact you by mind power."

"Sure now, and it's handicapped you are in such communication!"

"Please don't be angry," he said.

"Me? Angry? Why should I care if you go runnin' away to the south seas to get away from me?"

"Are you actually talking to me on the wirephone or are you in my mind?" Dylan asked.

"A little of each or neither," the girl said. "Me brother Shawn picked up the speaking tube in the constable's booth at the top of the ramp on Peach Grove Row and I'm talkin' into it from me temple by mind power."

"Isn't that a kind of roundabout way of doing things when you could contact my mind directly?"

"Oh no, I'd never! Some folks get very stuffy about havin' ladies in their minds. They're ashamed of what she might find out."

"Clarinda, I'm sorry if I hurt your feelings."

"How would the likes of the MacTague have feelin's that the likes of the MacBride could be hurtin'?"

"Darling, please, listen to me. I didn't mean to—"

" 'Each night through Loveland we'd wander, sweetheart /Tellin' love's story anew,' " the priestess sang in her soft, husky voice. " 'Out of a blue sky a dark cloud came rollin' '

/Breakin' my heart in two. . . .' "

"You're not listening," Dylan said, "to what I'm saying or to what I'm thinking."

"Sure now, and how would I be knowin' what you're thinkin' when you forbid me to even peek?"

"Then listen to me! I have something to ask you."

"Why, la, sir, I'd be most happy to accept your kind invitation to a canter along the Strand and a catered picnic," she said.

"Why, you little hussy, you've been picking my mind all the time!"

"Oh, I never!" she said. "You must have said it."

"I did not, and you—oh, never mind. You will come?"

"Dressed in me best and with me best foot forward."

"Very well. I'll send a hansom for you at six."

"No hackman would have the nerve to come down into Trogtown. Why don't I just fly straight into your bed at five-thirty instead? If I can remember the spell, that is."

"Clarinda, be serious. Wait at the ramp gate for the hansom."

"Ah, I like me idea the better," she said. "We could have an extra hour together, and love is what it's me business to be serious about."

"Please, Clarinda, be a good girl and—"

"Sure and who's better than me when I have to be? You make me very sad sometimes, laddie. 'Tis a sad fate for a fertility priestess to find herself in love with a cold-blooded Sassenach."

"Since when did the Saxons wear the kilt?" he parried.

She ignored that, determined to be sad. " 'All de world am sad and dreary, everywhere I roam/Oh, Troggies, how my heart grows weary/Far from de old folks at home.' "

"I'll see you in the morning," Dylan said.

"Be sure and tuck your head under the covers," she said, "lest some bad witch priestess kiss your chaste lips when you're never lookin'."

"Good night, love," he said and hung up.

Wrap your kilties tightly 'round your virtue, laddie, her mind voice continued to rag him. *Terrible things can happen to pretty Vineland byes in the dark o' the moon when witches ride bareback on the North Wind.*

Good night!

"Say, darlin', say/When I'm far away/Sometimes you

may think of me, dear," she was singing as he felt the soft fingers of her mind withdraw from his.

Dylan was shaking his head in exasperation as he went back to his charts, but while he worked his thoughts kept returning to the terrible days of the invasion of the Gogs. He remembered how he had first met the redheaded priestess of the almost extinct worship of Keridwen in her storefront temple on an ancient street in Trogtown. At that time he had fancied himself in love with Noel ap Lynn's sister, the lady Alice, but it hadn't taken long for the salty-tongued beauty to dissuade him of that fantasy and convince him there was only one woman in the world. But Clarinda was a problem and one he wasn't sure would be solved by marriage.

He thought of how brave she had been despite her loudly proclaimed cowardice during the dreadful days when Kar Kaballa's horsemen threatened the very existence of Avallon and the world. He remembered how, when he and his friends had fled before the advancing Gogs with the only Gatling gun on Annwn, he had been thrown into the path of the ghastly little horsemen. Clarinda had suddenly appeared between him and death with only a mop and a bucket of water as weapons. When he thought of all this and recalled how she had fought beside him on the walls of Avallon as the Gogs threw the Endless Storm against the city, how could he not love her?

And finally they had faced death together in the caves of Cythraul, Clarinda accompanying him despite her very genuine terror. She had teleported the dynamite they needed to blast the walls of the caves and let in the rivers of lava from the underground volcano to destroy the ageless terror of Cythraul.

She's a problem but she's a brave lass, he said to himself, pouring a nightcap and picking up a copy of *Scientific Avallon* to read in bed. *There's none you'd want better beside you in time of trouble.*

But what about the times when there was no trouble? A girl who is a good comrade at the crank of a Gatling gun on the walls of a besieged city is one thing, but a girl you can't take to the admiral's ball without being afraid she'll wreck the place is another. He'd never forget the ball Admiral McCracken had given in celebration of the delivery of the city from the Gogs. He had taken Clarinda of course, and there had been a certain Bishop Tishman present. The Anglic-Reform church bishop of Imola had waxed rather snide about the morals and divinity of Keridwen within the hearing of her priestess, and Dylan had watched in horror as the punch bowl had risen up into the air, seemingly of its own volition, and floated above the bishop. Then it had slowly tipped over, spilling punch, ice and fruit in a chilly cascade over the churchman's head.

The sight of a bishop in full robes, sputtering and spitting and trying to dislodge half an orange that had somehow stuffed itself into his mouth, was unnerving to say the least, especially to the young man who thought he knew what had caused the punch bowl's strange behavior.

"Clarinda, why did you do it?" Dylan had demanded after he had dragged her off into a corner.

"Do what, love?" The smile on the lovely face was angelic.

"You dumped the punch bowl on the bishop's head. Don't you have any manners?"

"And where were his manners, criticizin' another person's religion right in front of her?"

"He didn't know who you were. You were introduced as Miss Clarinda MacTague of the exarch of Hibernia, not as a priestess of Keridwen."

"Sure now, and if he belonged to a real religion, he wouldn't have to be told; he'd have the power and be able to see he was insultin' someone's religion."

"Well, you're criticizing his religion, aren't you?"

"Not a bit of it. That can't be a religion because it's got no spells and no powers. I'm not criticizin', just pointin' out."

"Well, at least he doesn't know who did it," Dylan said. "That's something to be thankful for."

"Oh, doesn't he now? You mean I forgot to sign the orange I jammed in his mouth? I should go back."

"No, Clarinda. That was a terrible thing to do at a formal ball."

"And who's to say I did it?" She grinned. "Can the likes of the MacTague help it if punch bowls have a mind to fly around and dump punch on a bald-headed ninny in women's skirts? Perhaps the strong stuff they put in the punch was to blame and it set the bowl off."

Shaking his head at the memory of the incident, Dylan leaned back on the pillows and opened the magazine. The first article that caught his attention was on astronomy and dealt with strange sightings on the planet Thor. Thor was the fourth planet of the system in which Annwn was the third. In some ways they were almost sister planets although Thor was thought by many savants to have little atmosphere or water. There had been speculation, however, that life might exist there. And now, according to the article, strange flashes of light had been seen on the so-called red planet by observers at the Emrys University Observatory. Mysterious clouds of smoke had also been seen passing across the face of the planet. Was it possible, the article asked, that there was another race of beings out there in the immensity of space? If so, was it possible that they were as civilized as the people of Annwn?

Dylan was at first inclined to reject the idea until he remembered that a few years ago he hadn't believed the tales about a world called Earth that existed on the other side of the Shimmering Gates. Then, in the days prior to the coming of the Gogs, he had met a man from that mythical world, a Major F. Woodrow Churchward, late of the First Voluntary Cavalry, who had come to him with a warning of the impending invasion and a weapon he claimed would help repel it.

No, Earth was no myth and neither were the Shimmering Gates which connected it with Annwn. Earth was a true twin of Annwn, existing in a different space-time continuum. The way between the worlds lay in the Green Dolphin Islands at a place called Caer Pendryvan, guarded by mysterious cowled creatures called the Guardians.

Of the Gates themselves, Churchward had told him, "They are not magic but science. The science of a race of beings more advanced than either Annwn or Earth. The Gates were created at a time in the past that our history doesn't remember, for a purpose I can't conceive. The beings who created them left the Guardians to watch over them and departed for places unknown on business unimaginable."

So if there were at least two worlds with intelligent beings living on them, Dylan asked himself, why couldn't there be intelligent creatures living on Thor as well? The people of Earth and Annwn were of one race, of course, and existed in a strange sort of symbiosis fueled by the secret trade in ideas and goods that continuously passed through the Gates. They shared not only a common heritage but common languages, although slightly altered on each world. In-

ventions, literature and music filtered through from one to
the other. Anything invented, written or composed on one
world was likely to show up on the other as a profitable
enterprise in the hands of some crafty entrepreneur.

Dylan! Dylan, me love! Clarinda's frightened voice
sounded in his mind. *It's all atremble I am from somethin'
awful I've seen! Come to me, darlin', please come to me!*

Dylan felt the terror in the girl's voice and he also felt
the strong tug of of her power. She had never used her
strange talent just this way before but he knew what it must
mean. He leaped from the bed and barely had time to pull
on his kilts to cover his nakedness before his room disappeared and he was standing in a small alcove in Clarinda's
apartment next to a life-size statue of Keridwen. Beyond
the hangings he could hear the perpetual uproar of the
dozen red-haired young devils who were the priestess's
younger brothers and sisters, but Clarinda was waiting for
him in the alcove.

Clarinda MacTague was almost as tall as Dylan, and even
the ill-fitting wrapper she wore couldn't disguise her god-
desslike figure. In the light from the votive lamp burning at
Keridwen's feet the girl's red hair glistened almost gold
and turned the violet pools of her eyes into dark, frightened
saucers above the upturned nose and wide sensuous mouth.

"Darlin', darlin', you came!" she cried, throwing herself
into his arms and pressing against him, trembling.

"I didn't have much choice," Dylan said, embarrassed by
his state of near nakedness and annoyed at the unceremo-
nious way he had been dragged from his bed and hurled
through space.

"Sure now, it was necessary or I'd never of done it,"
Clarinda said, shivering against him. "I was that frightened
I couldn't stand to be alone."

"What is it? What frightened you?"

Another shudder shook her. "Them things . . . the ones
you was readin' about."

"What? What things?" he asked, wondering if she'd been
nipping at the bottle of Hibernian whiskey he knew she kept
hidden behind the statue.

"Them creatures from that place called Thor, the ones
with the tentacles you was readin' about in that scientific
magazine."

"Have you been snooping around in my mind again?"

Dylan roared and then stopped to hold her off and stare at her. "What creatures from Thor with tentacles? The article I was reading said nothing about such creatures. It was just speculating that there *might* be some intelligent form of life on the fourth planet."

"Intelligent but horrible," Clarinda all but whimpered. "I wish to Keridwen I'd never looked!"

Dylan continued to stare at her in amazement. "You mean you used your power to look across millions of miles of space to see if there was life on Thor?"

She shook her head. "No, not the power." She pointed to the large shallow bowl sitting on her reading table. "The Cauldron of Keridwen."

Dylan strode over to the gold bowl, remembering the first time he had met the priestess and how they had gazed into the Cauldron together and seen their deaths in the caves of Cythraul.

"There's nothing there now," he said.

"It needs the elixir," she said, taking down a gold bottle and pouring a pale pink liquid into the bowl. She tried to smile and make light of it but her voice was shaking as she said, "There, now 'tis the Cauldron of Keridwen, or at least my small, economy version of it."

"It has no power," Dylan said. "You know yourself that it was wrong the last time. We didn't die."

"Aye, but we came close, love, so close I felt the sulfuric breath of Cythraul rufflin' me hair and I shiver every time I remember it."

"But the prophecy was wrong," Dylan insisted. "So why should you believe it this time?"

"Fate is fan-shaped," she said. "We saw what might have happened but didn't. That was in the future, but what I saw tonight was *now*, so it must be true. And terrible it was, I'm tellin' you! Big, grayish lumps the size of bears with hides that glistened like wet leather, and awful V-shaped mouths but no brows and no chins, just them bunches of tentacles."

She leaned forward to stir the pink liquid in the bowl, reciting the ritual words. "There are more worlds than in the Cauldron of Keridwen. . . . The bubbles are the worlds, and the bubbles are gathering . . . Annwn-Thor . . . Earth-Mars. . . . Look into the Cauldron, Dylan MacBride. What do you see?"

"Nothing," Dylan said. "I see nothing."

"Look again. The picture is forming . . . the vision is coming," she intoned, and then suddenly her face went chalky white and her hand moved toward her mouth as though to stifle the scream that burst from her lips seconds later. "No, no! Keridwen, no!"

She turned from the Cauldron sobbing and threw herself into Dylan's arms. "No, no, no! I can't bear it! It's worse than before!"

Dylan gathered the trembling girl close and tried to comfort her. "It's all right, darling, it's all right. Nothing can hurt you while I'm here. What was it you saw?"

"Its mind . . . I touched the mind of one of them things out there! One of them slimy things on that world they call Thor."

"Then they're not just blobs of protoplasm. Was its mind slimy too? Is that what terrified you?"

"No, not slimy. It was like . . . like a multiplication table come to life, logical, precise, cold. There was no emotion, no feelin's at all, just pure, hard logic. Oh, it was horrible, horrible! Hold me tight, darlin', I'm that terrified!"

Chapter 2

The next morning Clarinda arrived at the Strandside Riding Academy only forty-five minutes late, but the wait was worthwhile, Dylan decided, when he saw how stunning she looked. She was dressed in an expensive riding habit Dylan had once given her but which she had never worn before. It enhanced her striking figure admirably as she stepped from the hansom he had sent to fetch her.

He kissed her hand. "The goddess Diana dressed for the hunt."

"Oh, go on with you!" she said, dimpling roguishly. "And look at his lordship all decked out in top hat and pants for a change."

Dylan tilted the hat to one side and looked down at his taws with the MacBride tartan tucked neatly into his riding boots. "Well, you have to admit kilts are a little out of place on horseback."

She laughed. "And I was lookin' forward to seein' your skirt flyin' up over you head. 'Tis disappointed I am."

The groom came over then, leading Dylan's stallion and a spirited but gentle mare for the girl. Clarinda inspected her mount suspiciously. "Why is it built so high off the ground?"

Dylan smiled and led her closer to the horse. "That's the way nature created them."

She stared up at the mare uneasily. "And did they think to build a ladder to get up on top of them?"

"This is your ladder," Dylan said, showing her the stirrup. "Put your foot in this and swing yourself up onto the saddle."

"Oh, I never could! I'd just fall off the other side on me head. Why don't I work up a little spell and power meself up onto the beastie's back?"

"And let everyone at the club know you're a witch?"

"Would they disown you if they knew you had a witch for a ladylove?" she asked, reaching out to stroke the horse's velvety nose. Expecting a tidbit, the mare opened her mouth, and Clarinda jerked her hand back when she saw the big white teeth. "I thought horses was vegetarians."

"They are," Dylan said.

"Then what does it need teeth like that for?" she demanded.

"To bite into green apples and carrots," Dylan said. "I should have told you to bring some sugar cubes."

"Oh, is it sugar it likes? Well, let's see if we can find some." With all the gestures of a stage magician, the priestess reached out and plucked a lump of sugar from behind the animal's ear. "There you go, me beauty. You just didn't know where to look; you had sugar of your own all along."

The horse chomped happily on the sugar while Dylan helped the girl place her foot in the stirrup. She swing herself up into the saddle with a display of trim booted ankles and delightfully curved calves.

"Just relax," Dylan said, mounting his own horse. "The horse will do all the work."

They started off at a slow walk. "The things you get me

into, MacBride! Last night it was into the head of a beastie with a mind like an adding machine and today 'tis up on the back of a giant horse that'd just as soon gobble me up as it would that lump of sugar."

"Your horse is a mare and very gentle," Dylan said.

"So 'tis a lady horse. It'll be a good thing if she behaves like a lady," Clarinda said and then without realizing what she was doing touched her boots to the horse's sides. The animal broke into a trot and the priestess yelped. "It's runnin' away with me, Dylan! Help!"

"Just get a grip on the reins and hold her back," Dylan advised.

Clarinda gripped the reins as though her life depended on it. "Whoa! Slow down now, beastie, and walk nice or I'll cast a spell on you that will make your ears grow long and your whinny turn into a hee-haw."

When Clarinda and the mare had settled down and agreed to get along, Dylan led the way out onto the bridle path that led south along the bank of the Silver Strand. They followed the path through blooming oleander and jasmine that dotted the grassy embankment until they came to a small bridge across the South Canal. The far side of the canal was a semirural area with frequent clusters of summer cottages and an occasional villa in sight. Once they passed a large barge heading north on the canal, pulled by a team of oxen plodding along the tow path. The voice of the keel man floated back to them faintly as he sang, "Low bridge . . . fifteen years on the Great South Canal."

On the other side of them lay the broad expanse of the Silver Strand, as much as twenty miles wide in some places, in others only three or four. The estuary was filled with shipping, and a great white river steamer was heading downstream, paddle-wheels churning, decks crowded with excursioners and a band playing loudly.

Clarinda laughed and blew a kiss after the boat as the sound faded with its progress. " 'Tis a beautiful boat filled with happy people practicin' sweet love with Keridwen's blessin', and 'tis a lovely day as well."

"I can't argue with that," Dylan said, grinning. After the nights of fog and days of haze, the weather had cleared. A bright yellow sun was shining down, the water of the Strand sparkled and the sails of small craft and the smoke of steamers all seemed to add to the liveliness of the scene.

THE SECOND WAR OF THE WORLDS

He was glad he had suggested the outing. It was good to see Clarinda enjoying herself and apparently free of the fear that had plagued her the night before.

Clarinda's face clouded as she picked up his thought. "No, love, I've not forgotten them nasty things but as you kept tellin' me, they are forty million miles away."

"Forty-five million or so, and that's a long way for even the coldest of intellects."

"Then let's hope to Keridwen they stay there and leave us be."

"I don't see how they could do anything else," Dylan said. "That would be an impossibly long walk, even for creatures with a dozen tentacles."

"Them addin' machine minds could be buildin' a bridge that long if they decided to," Clarinda said.

They were nearing the docks and Dylan could see a peculiar looking craft with a small conning tower and a single smokestack tied up at the almost deserted pier the professor had specified.

"That has to be the *Thunderbolt*," Dylan said.

"Sure, and it's not a proper lookin' boat at all," Clarinda said, "or maybe it's turned turtle already and that's its bottom."

The odd-shaped craft was about fifty feet long and had a beam of perhaps ten or twelve at its widest. Several men were visible around her, including a gentleman in a top hat and a white duster standing on the deckhouse waving to them.

"Mr. MacBride, sir, is it that you have arrived?" he shouted in Lombosa's peculiar accent. "We are all but making ready for the test to begin." He scrambled down from the deckhouse and hurried toward them. "If you and the lady will but come on deck, the ship she will part lines from the dock." Lombosa was a tall, gangling man with a thin black mustache and pince-nez. He bowed formally to Clarinda and shook hands with Dylan.

"The lady will do nothin' of the kind," Clarinda said. "Nothin' could get me on that iron sinkin' boat."

"But, madonna, it is a diving boat, not a sinking boat," Lombosa protested.

"One will get you five that sinkin' is the proper word," the redhead said, staring past him at the clumsy craft.

"Perhaps it is that my Anglic is not right," the professor

said, taking off his top hat and replacing it with a motoring cap turned backward and a pair of goggles. "One must prepare for spray and the strong wind of speed such as in a motorcar."

Dylan was inspecting the *Thunderbolt* more closely and was dismayed to see that, just sitting there at the dock with all lines pulled taut, it appeared to be listing a little and the gentle waves of the estuary washed over its deck near the bow.

"Is this the first time you have—" Dylan's question was interrupted by the sound of galloping hooves and a woman's voice calling for help.

They all turned to stare as a dark-haired young woman dashed by on the back of a chestnut-colored horse with reins trailing. The girl's hat was gone, hair blowing in the wind as she clung to the mane of the runaway and called again, "Help! Please, somebody help!"

Dylan swung up into the saddle. "I'll go. She might be killed."

"Bide your time, love," Clarinda advised. "The horse will tire itself out and stop after a bit."

Lombosa added his protests, but Dylan ignored them both and set off after the runaway. It took only a few minutes for his stronger, faster mount to overtake the chestnut, then he grabbed the reins and forced the animal to a halt.

"Thank you, sir," the girl gasped, pushing lustrous black hair back from her face.

Dylan found himself staring into cool gray eyes that held no fear. She was slightly breathless but unafraid, and he found himself admiring the delicate curve of cheek, the thin aquiline nose and small rounded chin. The firm, full lips parted in a grateful smile, showing even white teeth.

"I don't know what I would have done if you hadn't come to my aid. I don't usually lose the reins that way but this pesky beast was startled by the air horn of a steamer up the channel. He reared and almost threw me off before beginning his mad dash."

The woman spoke with a faint accent, not as though Anglic were foreign to her but as though she came from a part of the world where it was spoken with a different dialect. It in no way detracted from the rich, husky voice or her aristocratic bearing and manner.

She extended a slender white hand. "To whom am I indebted for my limbs, if not my life?"

"I am Dylan MacBride of Shetland Head, Vineland."

"A Highlander . . . how interesting!" she said. "I had noticed your plaid."

"The tartan of Clan MacBride," he acknowledged.

"Let me see," she said, putting a finger to her pretty chin in an attitude of thinking. "Oh, yes. A duchy on the east coast of this continent, divided from the mainland by a series of great rivers, and ruled by a duke of the same name as yourself. Are you of the ducal family, then?"

"Only a cousin," Dylan said. "My father was an explorer, the younger son of the present duke's grandfather. I follow in my father's footsteps."

"How fascinating! You must meet my uncle, Professor Philander. He teaches ethical culture at Ogmios University here in the city, but is also interested in the natural sciences. If he were here, he would introduce me as the Lady Philippa, newly arrived in your beautiful and ancient city of Avallon from my home in—" the lady's gray eyes grew brighter and Dylan was conscious of the faintest feathery feeling in his mind. Then the glow faded from her eyes and she finished her sentence—"from my home in Meropis."

Dylan was surprised. Meropis was one of the few areas on the planet of which he was almost totally ignorant. Why, he wasn't even sure that Anglic was spoken there.

"You will come to meet my uncle so that the head of the family can thank you properly, won't you, Mr. MacBride?"

"Well, of course, I—" Dylan suddenly became aware of two spots of fire on the back of his head and turned quickly to find Clarinda seated on her horse very straight and stiff within a few paces of them. "Oh, I didn't hear you ride up. Clarinda, this is Lady Philippa . . ." He stopped in confusion and turned back to the dark-haired woman. "I'm sorry, but I didn't catch your last name, your ladyship."

"It's Dunnmuir," Clarinda said quickly. "Lady Philippa Dunnmuir of Meropis, or so she says."

Dylan looked from one to the other before continuing the introduction. "Lady Philippa, this is Miss Clarinda MacTague."

"Pleased to meet you," Clarinda said, with the same enthusiasm she would have greeted a rattlesnake in her bed.

"And I am pleased to meet such a charming young lady,"

the other girl said. "What beautiful red hair, and with the peaches-and-cream complexion, you must be from—"

"Hibernia," Clarinda said. "Me father's a pugilist and me mither a fish peddler."

"Both professions of great mystical power," Dylan said hastily, "as Clarinda has told me many times."

"It was magical potency I mentioned," Clarinda corrected him.

"Yes, and you've inherited their powers, haven't you, Miss MacTague?" Lady Philippa said, smiling slightly as she stared into the hostile violet eyes. "There is an aura about you, an aura of power."

"I have the *tag hairn,* the *fith-fath* and the *sian,*" Clarinda said. "I'm of the Gwyllian, a prophetic sisterhood. I can do a lot of things . . . once in a while."

"How fascinating. I have friends who would die to meet you."

"It might not kill 'em," Clarinda said ungraciously, "but they could come away with a few warts."

Lady Philippa threw her head back and laughed, but Dylan was embarrassed.

"Clarinda isn't really a witch," he said. "Actually, she's a priestess of Keridwen."

"Yes, I know," Lady Philippa said, "and Keridwen is the Cymru goddess of love, isn't she?"

"She's the mother of them all," Clarinda said. "The most important of the elder gods. But she's not above teachin' the likes of me some fine spells for warts on the skin and spiders in the hair."

Lady Philippa's merry, tinkling laugh rang out again and she turned to Dylan, offering him her hand. "I want to thank you again, Mr. MacBride, and renew my invitation. My uncle is entertaining at a soiree tomorrow afternoon. Please come, and bring Miss MacTague with you."

"I'd be delighted," Dylan said, ignoring the glare he got from Clarinda.

"See you then," Lady Philippa said and turned to ride away. She stopped to stare at a hillock on the far side of the South Canal before turning to Dylan again. "Are you aware that someone is watching you, Mr. MacBride?"

Dylan looked in the direction she indicated and saw two figures outlined against the morning sun. One was a very tall, thin figure in a deerstalker cap and opera coat, the other shorter and more robust looking. He couldn't make out the faces because the light was behind them, but he could see that the tall man raised a pair of field glasses to his eyes and appeared to be studying them.

"They do seem to be looking this way," Dylan said, "but there is no reason anyone would watch me. My plans to explore the Ice Caves are common knowledge and I can't think of—"

"Sure now, and maybe they're bird-watchin'," Clarinda said with a fleeting glance in Lady Philippa's direction, "or watchin' one fancy bird, anyway."

"They are spies!" Professor Lombosa had come up behind them, breathing heavily from his walk. "They have been sent to steal the secrets of my iron boat and my nonlethal poisonous dart gun! They are from Thunderania and would use my inventions against the Empire!"

"Well, we can't have the goose-stepping Thunderanians getting their hands on such deadly weapons and destroying the Empire, can we, Mr. MacBride?" Lady Philippa asked, laughing. "So I'll leave you to view the good professor's magic and be on my way."

She waved and rode off, leaving Dylan wondering how she had known he'd come to see Lombosa's craft in action.

"Come, we must be away!" the professor urged. "We must hasten before the spies and their confederates can interfere."

Dylan looked again at the two men on the hillock and from the way they were standing now, he was almost certain they were watching neither him nor Lombosa's invention but Lady Philippa as she rode back toward the city.

"Perhaps there's a mystery about the lovely lady," he mused.

"You keep away from that black-haired witch! She's one of them brainy ones for sure, and she'll bring you a year's worth of trouble in a day!"

"Is that a prediction or just wishful thinking?" Dylan asked.

"I've seen it," Clarinda said. "It hurts me head but I've seen it."

"Mr. MacBride, the tide . . . the tide!" Professor Lombosa said.

"Yes, what about it?"

"The engines would be better if we go upstream with the tide and drift back down. You and the lady will come aboard now, perhaps it is so?"

But Clarinda had something else on her mind. "Are you goin' to her fancy soiree?"

"She invited both of us," Dylan said.

"She *invited* you," Clarinda sniffed. "She just threw me in for the sound of it."

"The tide makes," Lombosa said.

"She's a clever one despite bein' a Sassenach, and she's got a little of the power."

Dylan's eyes widened. Now he knew why Clarinda had spoken openly of her powers. She wasn't exactly ashamed of them but she seldom mentioned them before strangers. Had her words been intended as a warning to Lady Philippa?

"Look, Mr MacBride, you can see perhaps the little ripples on the water? The tide is going and we should go also, is it not so?"

"Yes, we might as well," Dylan said. "Are you sure you don't want to join us, darling?"

"I'll stay with me two feet on firm earth and watch the sinkin' boat sink," the girl said. "And if you drown, it'll serve you right for makin' goo-goo-eyes at the black-headed Sassenach witch!"

"She said she was from Meropis," Dylan said.

"I know, but there's somethin' in me that says different."

"Please, please, we must hurry or we will not have the tide," Lombosa pleaded.

They had been walking back toward the dock as they talked and now Dylan looped the reins of the two horses to a hitching post and followed Lombosa aboard the ungainly craft. He stood by the conning tower as the crew of four let go fore and aft. Lombosa went through the hatch in the side of the tower and up a ladder to the small bridge where a helmsman stood at the wheel.

"Let go all lines," Lombosa ordered. "All engines back one-third. Sound one long blast on the air horn."

The *Thunderbolt* gave a little jerk but didn't really back down. It just kind of drifted away from the pier as the engines began to hum fitfully.

Clarinda waved from the dock. "Don't be gettin' your feet wet, love!"

Dylan smiled and waved and then realized that his feet were already wet. He looked down and saw water lapping over the low gunwales of the ram.

"Mr. Dylan, come into the conning tower," the professor called. "I will show you how this great vessel is steered."

Dylan bent over and stepped through the hatch to the tower. Standing on open grillwork above him were the inventor and the helmsman. Lombosa was talking into the speaking tube to the engine room.

"We are not moving. More power! Keep the engines running. What? What do you mean there's a foot of water in the engine room? How can there be? We're not diving."

Dylan heard the sound of running water and looked through the hatchway that led below. Water was pouring down into what must be the crew's quarters from an opening aft.

"Professor Lombosa," he called up to the inventor, "someone must have forgotten to secure a hatch over the air vent back aft."

Lombosa shrugged unconcernedly. "Oh yes, the hatch is loose. There is something wrong with the bolt that dogs it down. It is one of the little matters that must be tended to before perfection is attained."

"Well, I'd say it was pretty important," Dylan said, "because you're shipping water fast."

"No matter," Lombosa said. "It will take care of itself at a later time. More power, engine room, more power!"

The engines were making a frightful racket and the whole craft vibrated but was barely moving. In fact, the ship seemed to be drifting backward. It was also listing more than ever to starboard and, judging from the way the helmsman was tugging at the wheel, it wasn't responding.

"Starboard hard rudder it is," Lombosa said.

"Starboard hard, sir," the helmsman said and swung the wheel. The *Thunderbolt* shivered all over and started swinging slowly . . . but to port, not starboard.

They were almost in the middle of the channel now, about equidistant from either shore, and Dylan was becoming increasingly uneasy. More and more water was pouring through the defective hatch and occasionally water lapped over the coping of the hatch he was standing by as well.

"Professor, I think you should be wise to start your pumps."

Lombosa looked down at him in bewilderment. "Pumps? What pumps?"

"You mean you don't have pumps to eliminate water that

is shipped aboard?"

"Oh, those pumps. No. They are another matter that will be taken care of when perfection comes."

"Then I suggest you steer for shallow water at once," Dylan said.

"But it is no. We cannot test the diving in shallow water," Lombosa protested. "We need deep water for that."

"If you try to dive this thing in its present condition, I'll jump overboard and swim for it," Dylan said.

Lombosa looked more bewildered than before. "But how can you see the success of the test if you are in the water? It is much better to observe from on board."

A steamer standing down the estuary passed them about two hundred feet to starboard, sounding her air horn loudly and urgently. Men were wig-wagging from its deck and an officer on the bridge with a megaphone shouted across the water to them. "Do you require assistance?"

"Assistance? Of course not," Lombosa said indignantly. "We are even now getting up steam."

The steamer's wake hit them, and the ram put her sharp nose down into it. As Dylan watched, green water covered the whole ship forward of the conning tower. For one wild moment, he thought the ship was going to go down like the rock she seemed, but with a shudder she recovered and staggered along again at something under two knots.

"Professor Lombosa, if you don't put about and make for shallow water, you are going to drown us all!" Dylan shouted as he mounted the ladder to the steering platform and stood beside the helmsman. "This craft is sinking!"

"But that is impossible," the inventor said. "It is as steady as a rock. It is a craft of great—"

A stern-wheel paddleboat was passing close to them, sending out miniature breakers in all directions. One of them hit the *Thunderbolt* and she rolled over almost onto her beam ends.

"Get your crew topside, Lombosa!" Dylan yelled, grabbing the helm. "This thing is going to sink!"

"No, it is seaworthy for any purpose. We just need more power from the engine room."

An oil-covered face poked up through the hatch below. "The boilers are flooded, sir. There's three feet of water in the engine room and we're shipping more every minute."

"Get back to your post at once!" Lombosa ordered.

"Have you no courage? Relight the boilers and get up power!"

"Don't be an idiot!" Dylan said. "Get your crew topside at once! I'm making for shallow water with what way we still have left."

The ram answered the helm with a frightening sluggishness, but Dylan managed to bring her around with the help of the tide and the push of the wake of the paddle-wheel steamer. He pointed her sharp bow for the nearby mudflats.

The crew was scrambling out of the hatch below, crowding out on deck and ready to jump for it. Water was now starting to pour into that hatch as well as the one aft. If that kept up, the *Thunderbolt* would never make the mudflats.

"Dog down that hatch, damn it!" Dylan bellowed at the men below. "Hurry or it'll be too late!"

Somewhat reluctantly, two men closed the hatch and began to dog it. The *Thunderbolt* rolled starboard and fell back into the trough of a wave from the steamer's wake and wallowed along a little further. Dylan strained at the helm to keep her bow pointed toward shore, as she tended to turn broadside to the flats. Finally, with a tremendous shudder, he felt her touch bottom, slide through the soft mud for a few feet and settle with her decks barely awash.

"My beautiful ship, my great invention! What have you done with her?" Lombosa cried in despair. "You have wrecked her on a sandbar! I am ruined!"

"I have beached her, mister," Dylan said crisply. "As any proper sailor would have done with a sinking vessel under like circumstances."

"But she is sunk! I am ruined! You have sunk my powerful ram in the mud!"

Dylan ignored the hysterical man and climbed down from the steering platform and went out of the conning tower to examine the possibilities of wading ashore. Clarinda was running along the embankment, riding skirt held up about her pretty knees and hair streaming behind her like a red banner.

"Dylan, me love, are you all right?" she shouted.

"I'm fine," he told her, "but your prediction of getting my feet wet has certainly come true."

"Sure now, and it'll be more than your feet!" She was laughing at his plight now that she knew he was safe. "You'll be gettin' them pretty striped britches wet too, unless you're plannin' on takin' them off and carryin' them while I hide me face modestly."

Behind Dylan, Lombosa was berating the crew. "Dumbheads! Idiots! Incompetents! Why did you let the boiler fire go out? Why did you let the water leak in?"

Dylan scrambled down the sloping side of the ram and found himself in waist-deep water and mud up to his ankles. Slowly and laboriously he started to wade through the sludge toward the shore about forty feet away while Clarinda stood on the bank watching, hands on hips and eyes dancing with devilment.

"If only you were wearin' your skirts today, maybe they would bellow out and let you float ashore."

When Dylan just kept on plodding toward her without comment, she tried another tack. "I told you that woman would bring a year's worth of bad luck in a day, didn't I now? There's a geas on all them skinny little bustle-twitching hoity-toities!"

Dylan was in no mood for her teasing. He was already put out about getting his brand-new taws ruined. It had cost him a pretty penny to have them made up in the MacBride tartan and now they'd probably never be clean again because of the oily mud. Having Clarinda exercise her sharp sense of humor at his expense was too much.

"You might at least offer to give me a hand up the bank," he said when he was close to shore.

"Sure and you never saw the day when a MacTague wouldn't give a MacBride a helpin' hand," she said and reached out to him.

Dylan grasped her hand firmly and pulled. The girl came tumbling in on top of him and they both sank in the muddy water and came up spitting. Clarinda let out a howl like a banshee, swung a roundhouse blow that nearly knocked him down again and disappeared, leaving him standing in the water listening to Lombosa screech imprecations at his crew while the *Thunderbolt* settled deeper into the mud. The final insult came when the mud that had covered Clarinda for a few seconds and then hung in midair when she vanished suddenly gathered itself into a sloppy glob and hit him in the face.

Chapter 3

Dylan was sitting in an easy chair, nursing a hot toddy and hoping it would ward off the cold his sniffles seemed to indicate imminent, when the maid knocked on his door to announce that Major Churchward and another gentleman were at the outside door. Having shared adventures with Churchward during the terrible days when Kar Kaballa led his Gogs to the very gates of Avallon, it was with pleasure that Dylan told the woman to show the gentlemen in and fix two more drinks.

Churchward, a tall, robust man with a walrus mustache and a bluff manner, shook hands warmly. The ex-soldier of fortune, a former resident of Earth and onetime member of Teddy Roosevelt's Rough Riders, had been morose and at loose ends lately but now he was excited as he introduced the shorter, somewhat more portly man who appeared to be in his middle forties.

"Dylan MacBride, I want you to meet a gentleman who by reason of the delicacy of his mission on Annwn can be known only as Dr. W."

"Then he is from your world?" Dylan smiled as he shook hands with the newcomer.

"Yes, from beyond the Shimmering Gates," Churchward admitted and then fell silent as the maid entered with their drinks.

When his guests were comfortably seated and sipping appreciatively at the toddies, Dylan addressed the ruddy-faced man from Earth. "Are you a doctor of philosophy, sir?"

"No, of medicine, but I no longer practice that profession," Dr. W. said.

"Dr. W.'s mission to Annwn is of urgent importance," Churchward said. "One might say it is a matter of life or death for Earth and its twin."

Dylan's tone was slightly skeptical. "You mean there is a

31

menace that threatens both?"

"Most assuredly," Dr. W. said, "and it threatens the human race itself, Mr. MacBride."

Dylan looked from the doctor to Churchward and back again. Churchward was a sensible fellow, and the wild tale he had told on coming to Annwn had turned out to be simple truth, so perhaps it would be wise to at least hear his friend out.

"Tell your story, Doctor," Churchward said.

"Yes, yes," Dr. W. said, tugging at his mustache as Churchward freshened his drink from the gasogene that stood on the sideboard. "Let me see . . . where to begin?"

"The beginning would probably be best," Dylan said. "Especially if it is going to strain my credulity."

"Yes. Well, sir, two years ago, after Churchward had left Earth, our planet was struck by a terrible curse, a catastrophe unparalleled in its history, except perhaps for the onslaught of the Dark Ages."

"Was it a natural disaster?" Dylan asked as the man paused as though remembering events he preferred to forget.

"Natural? You could call it that, I suppose, if you consider the attempted destruction of one race of intelligent beings by another part of the process of natural selection."

"There was an invasion from Mars," Churchward broke in excitedly. "At about the same time we were fighting off the Gogs, Earth was struck by a devastating invasion from the planet Mars."

"Mars?" Dylan felt a chill as he remembered the article he had read in *Scientific Avallon* and Clarinda's frightening vision.

"Yes. The fourth planet of our system, which is about fifty million miles from Earth, is called Mars."

"Thor," Dylan said.

Dr. W. and Major Churchward looked at each other in surprise.

"Mars is to Thor what Earth is to Annwn," Dylan said.

"Yes, the doctor said, "and the analogy is even closer, but let me go on. Some dozen capsules fired from a giant cannon on Mars struck Earth in the middle of the English countryside. Before effective resistance could be organized, the giant squidlike creatures had managed to build——"

"Did you say squidlike?" Dylan interrupted. "With perhaps a dozen tentacles?"

"Yes," Dr. W. said. "Why do you ask?"

Dylan glanced at Churchward. "A friend of mine who has certain powers had a vision something like that."

"Clarinda," Churchward guessed.

"Yes," Dylan said, "but do go on with your story, Doctor."

"Yes. Well, the creatures built huge metal battle machines in which they could stride across the countryside. Using heat-rays and poisonous black smoke they destroyed the land armies of Great Britain, seized London and other large cities and advanced to the channel. There they were halted momentarily by the ironclads of the channel fleet but it seemed only a matter of time before they would be able to cross the water and begin the conquest of Europe. Once they had accomplished that, the world would have been theirs, the conquered human race kept alive only to serve as food for the victorious invaders."

"But that didn't happen or you wouldn't be here," Dylan said. "The conquest was never completed, was it?"

"No, because just when the Martians were preparing to build flying machines so they could drive off or sink the ironclads that held them in England, they were attacked by an enemy which apparently they never knew existed— Earth's microbes. The circumstances have still not been explained of how the microbes struck so suddenly and devastatingly that every Martian on Earth was dead within a fortnight but we do know that the germs which have plagued man for millennia destroyed his newer and more terrible enemy almost overnight."

"A miracle," Churchward said, "an absolute miracle."

"Yes, in a way you might say that," Dr. W. agreed, "but even though the enemy was destroyed on Earth, the menace still exists. For a reason never fully understood, only a limited number of capsules were fired from the great gun on Mars. It has been speculated that there was some accident to the monstrous weapon and that someday it might be repaired. Then we would again face a seemingly unstoppable enemy."

"And that's what you meant by a menace to both Earth and Annwn?" Dylan asked.

"Yes, Mr. MacBride, we now believe we may be faced with another Martian invasion."

"And you've come to Annwn to ask for help against that

invasion?"

The doctor sighed, took out his pipe and stuffed tobacco into it before he spoke again. "No, sir, we have not come to Annwn for help against an invasion of Earth. We are here to warn you that Annwn is the world about to be invaded."

"My God!" Dylan said. "What would lead you to a conclusion like that?"

"Mr. MacBride, after the defeat of the Martians, Earth science took a remarkable leap forward. The examination of their machines added immeasurably to our knowledge of many things, and one of those was optics. With principles learned from them, our savants made a much closer study of the planet Mars. We are now able to see the surface of that world more clearly than we were able to see our own moon before the invasion. What our astronomers have learned has convinced them that Mars never contained life but that the beings we called Martians were actually from someplace else. There was no evidence of science or civilization except for one large base where the space gun was installed. Even that is now deserted. But our scientists can make out a mysterious radiance nearby. Those few who know of the existence of Annwn believe it to be a gateway from Mars to Thor: in other words, the Shimmering Gates between those twin worlds. It now appears certain that the invasion of Earth originated on Thor, that Mars was used merely as a stepping-stone in space."

"Why?" Dylan asked, getting up to refill his mug. "If those creatures live in our system rather than yours, and I'm willing to concede they do from independent confirmation, why did they strike Earth first instead of Annwn?"

"We don't know for sure," Dr. W. said, "but from what Major Churchward tells me of your world and its mysticism, it may be that they thought Earth an easier target and planned a later invasion of Annwn through the Shimmering Gates. It may even be that they feared Cythraul."

"I see. So now you think they will attack Annwn. But Annwn shares Earth's microbes, Doctor, so won't they be faced with the same fate here as on Earth?"

The doctor puffed busily on his pipe, studying Dylan through the smoke. "They will indeed, if they haven't discovered some way of coping with the microbes. We have reason to believe, however, that the Martians have now been warned about the bacteria and will come prepared to deal with it."

Dylan stared at him. "How can you possibly know that?"

The Terran smiled rather grimly. "Because we have learned of the existence of a group which calls itself the Circle of Life, a cult which holds that the Martians are superior beings to men and as such, by the rules of evolution, deserve to survive more than mankind does."

"Extraordinary!" Dylan said.

"Elementary, my dear MacBride," Dr. W. replied. "At first the group was thought to be just one more eccentric cult that sprang up after the invasion, but after extensive investigation by my colleague, it was learned that this one was much more dangerous than the rest. One of the members is not only a brilliant scientist but is also a veritable Napoleon of crime as well. The others are fanatics but clever and able. My colleague, the world's foremost consulting detective, has determined that the Circle of Life not only believes the Martians more fit to survive than the human race but they are actually doing everything in their not inconsiderable power to bring this about."

Dylan shook his head. "It's almost unbelievable the lengths to which some people will go for their beliefs."

"Yes, isn't it? Within the last fortnight, my colleague has learned that most of the leaders of the Circle of Life have disappeared from their usual haunts. The Science Council believes they have somehow established communication across space with the Martians. My friend has confirmed this and further states that the Circle has informed the Martians of Earth-Annwn bacteria, told them how to combat it and offered aid in the coming invasion. Some cult members, in fact, have made their way through the Shimmering Gates to prepare the way for them."

"My God, sir, is this possible?" Dylan got to his feet to pace up and down.

"I'm afraid so," Dr. W. said. "As you may have guessed, my colleague and I are in the employ of the Science Council, which has been so effective in rebuilding a shattered Earth and advancing its knowledge. As soon as it was ascertained that the leadership of the Circle of Life was indeed on Annwn, I was dispatched immediately to this planet to spread the word of alarm. I contacted Major Churchward, since he was the only trustworthy Terran known to us who was resident in Avallon. Because you have contacts in both the military and scientific community, he suggested we come to you first."

"But it's so unbelievable."

"Many thought the Gogs were unbelievable," Churchward pointed out.

"Yes, and you'll remember how difficult it was to convince anyone of the dangers presented by a race of creatures already known in our history. How do you think they'll react to an unknown race millions of miles away?"

"I believe, sir," Dr. W. said, "that conclusive evidence of the coming invasion will soon be visible to your astronomers. When the great gun on Mars fired its first missiles Earthward, the explosions were seen by Earth astronomers. Your telescopes should be no poorer than ours were before the invasion; with foreknowledge of what to look for, your savants will be able to interpret what they see with their own eyes."

"Did seeing the invaders blast off do any good on your world, Doctor?"

"No, but your scientists will have the advantage of having read the history of our invasion, an excellent work called *The War of the Worlds,* by Mr. H. G. Wells. Your military men will be able to figure out how best to counteract the devastating power of the would-be conquerors." The doctor paused and took a book from his jacket pocket and handed it to Dylan. "I took the precaution of bringing a copy with me. I don't believe it is available in your book stores, is it?"

Dylan took the volume and leafed through it. "No, I've never seen it, and that's rather strange because there are other books by this gentleman for sale on Annwn. Of course, they are what he called scientific romances and this is a history of actual events, but if they were brought through the Shimmering Gates, why not this?"

"The Circle of Life is powerful," the doctor said, "and has many agents."

Churchward stirred restlessly. "What can we do to block this sinister plot? Alerting the authorities through this book or by word of mouth may be a lengthy process. Isn't there something we could be doing in the meantime to thwart the plans of the Circle of Life?"

"That is another of the reasons I have come to you gentlemen," the doctor said, relighting his pipe. "Several of the cult's members are right here in Avallon, while the rest have established a colony somewhere in the densely wooded interior of the continent, the area which is called Trans-Mortania, I believe."

"That's right," Churchward said. "It's the Far West of this continent."

Dr. W. nodded and leaned forward in his chair to say earnestly, "The first thing we must do is get close to known cult members in the city, learn as much as we can about their plans, especially the exact location of their colony, because that is almost certainly the place they expect the Martians to land. That is where you can be of great help, Mr. MacBride."

"I can?" Dylan asked in surprise. "How?"

"By expanding an acquaintanceship that already exists. You were observed in conversation with one of the inner circle members of the group."

Dylan stared at the man. "I was? I *know* one of these people? Are you sure?"

"Yes. This morning, out along the Silver Strand near the Old South Docks, you were talking to Lady Philippa Dunnmuir, were you not?"

Dylan nodded slowly. "Then you were one of the men on the hill with the binoculars and it was the lady you were watching."

"Indeed, yes. She has been under observation since she arrived here last week. We know she will eventually contact the other members and lead us to them, but time may be running out, and that is why we hope you will be willing to cultivate her friendship and find out all you can about the Circle of Life and their hidden colony."

Dylan started to pace again. "I don't believe I care for this at all, sir," he said. "What you're suggesting is that I spy on a lady, and I find that most distasteful."

"What I'm suggesting, Mr. MacBride," the doctor said with some asperity, "is that the lady is into a very dirty business, one which might mean the extermination of the human race. Under such circumstances, the ordinary rules of civility and chivalry must be set aside."

"But Lady Philippa comes from a good family," Dylan argued. "She is intelligent as well as attractive. She could not possibly be involved with a gang of desperate plotters ... anarchists who conspire to destroy mankind."

Dr. W. sighed deeply and laid aside his pipe. "All the people we have identified as members of the Circle of Life come from good families. Only one has any kind of criminal background. They are all bright, well-to-do, socially acceptable people, but they are also fanatics."

Dylan shook his head. "I just can't accept that."

"Perhaps the lady is innocently involved," Churchward suggested. "A pawn in the hands of unscrupulous conspirators."

"Perhaps," Dr. W. said but his tone was dubious. "She is one of the most outspoken of the whole group concerning the moral and intellectual superiority of the Martians, of their greater fitness to survive . . . but perhaps she doesn't fully understand what the fate of the human race would be in the event of a Martian conquest."

Churchward turned to Dylan. "It would not be dishonorable to at least sound out the lady."

Dylan agreed reluctantly. "All right. She invited me to a soiree at her uncle's house tomorrow. I'll at least keep my ears open."

"Good! That's all we ask," the doctor said and rose to leave. "By the way, Mr. MacBride, we understand you have an interest in an ironclad diving ram called the *Thunderbolt*."

"An interest?" Dylan laughed. "I'd be interested in seeing it condemned as a death trap. I got soaked to the skin and ruined my new riding clothes by just looking at it."

"Hmm," the doctor said. "We were wondering if it might not be a good means of transportation in our search for the Martian landing area. We could perhaps approach unseen."

"You'd be more likely to get yourselves drowned," Dylan said.

Dr. W. looked disappointed. "Are you sure it's totally worthless?"

"Well, perhaps not totally," Dylan conceded. "The concept is good, I believe, but the craft is dreadfully under-engined and needs increased stability and a higher freeboard. If those things were taken care of and attention was given to waterproofing the hatch ventilator covers, she might possibly be able to navigate the Silver Strand and lakes and rivers, but I just don't see any way she could be made fit for the high seas or for exploration of the sort I plan."

"Interesting, most interesting," the doctor said. "It will

bear looking into at least."

After his two visitors had departed, Dylan sat brooding about the fantastic story Dr. W. had told. He wondered what part this alleged menace might play in his plans to explore the Ice Caves. Somehow he didn't feel very optimistic that his expedition would get under way this time either.

Chapter 4

The affair at Professor Philander's rented town house was on an unusually high intellectual plane. Philosophers, natural scientists, theologians, mystics and scholars of every breed seemed to be present. In spite of the fact that he was dressed as elegantly as any man there in his cutaway coat, kilts and top hat, Dylan felt out of place. His small fame as an explorer had been expanded by his active participation in the Goggish War and this had gained him admiring recognition in military and political circles, but he felt completely out of his element among these deep thinkers and high-blown talkers who had come to do honor to Philander and his niece, Lady Philippa.

So he just tried to stay out of everybody's way and listen politely to whomever was nearby while balancing a cup of tea and nibbling at a dainty morsel called a tea sandwich. He didn't mind being left to himself. He had something of his own to think about. On the way over, the driver of the hansom cab had made such a nuisance of himself that Dylan had become suspicious. The man was odd-looking to start with, tall and lean and dressed in a straw hat and top coat with a cape-like back. Bewhiskered and garrulous, the hackman had commented on the weather, discussed the upcoming parliamentary elections and went on at length about the fact that the fourth planet, Thor, was very bright in the sky of late.

Dylan had been noncommittal about each subject in turn but now he wondered what the man was up to. Was he a spy for the mysterious Circle of Life perhaps? He dismissed that as nonsense, telling himself he was getting as paranoid as that idiot Lombosa. Why would the Circle of Life be spying on him? Surely they couldn't know about the doctor from Earth who had contacted him. Then he remembered that Clarinda had said something about Lady Philippa having the power. If that was true, she already knew everything about him, including what he was thinking.

Sure now, you're not thinkin' I'd be lettin' that hussy pick your brains! Clarinda's mind was touching his. *That would be worse than havin' you lallygagging with her.*

I have no intention of lallygagging with Lady Philippa, Dylan thought back indignantly, *and I'm sure she feels the same way about me. She is not only beautiful but intelligent, idealistic and serious-minded—definitely not the lallygagging type."*

Oh, so 'tis intelligent and serious-minded she is! And that, I suppose, would be makin' her a lot different from the silly little flibbertigibbets you're used to, includin' yours truly!

Dylan clenched his jaw in exasperation, as he so often did during an exchange with Clarinda. Without seeming to try, she could bemuse and befuddle him until he wasn't sure what he was saying, or thinking either.

He tried to start over. *Clarinda, I didn't mean I thought you were any less beautiful or intelligent, compared to her. After all, no one would ever mistake her for a goddess, and quite a few people, myself included, have commented many times on your striking resemblance to Keridwen.*

Go on with you! I've no time for your blarney, especially since you're half Sassenach and do it so badly!

Well, I'm making progress, Dylan thought. *That's the first time you've ever admitted I'm at least half Cymric.*

I'm admittin' nothin' of the kind! I don't know what the other half of you is . . . some peculiar kind of heathen, no doubt.

You're a fine one to call me a heathen! What about all those things your precious Keridwen is rumored to do?

There you go, makin' fun of me religion again! Have you no respect for anything?

Dylan sighed. Clarinda MacTague could go on all night this way, and he didn't have all night. He had the feeling people were looking at him a little oddly already, probably because of the varying expressions that crossed his face or perhaps because he moved his lips when he tried to hold one of these long-distance arguments with the witch-priestess.

Sure now, and I'm wearyin' your mind," she said with mock sympathy. *Or is it that you want to get rid of me so you can hold hands with the black-haired wench? Well, me mither warned me that if you let a man take advantage of you, he'll lose all respect and five minutes later go chasin' off after some skinny bustle-twitcher!*

Clarinda, I have never—

And you better not be thinkin' about it neither! If you lay one hand on that connivin' Earth wench, I'll put a geas on you that'll turn you into a frog!

Then she was gone from Dylan's mind, leaving him as puzzled as he was irritated. Clarinda had said "Earth wench." Lady Philippa had told them she was from Meropis, and there was only one place Clarinda could have gotten different information: from Lady Philippa's mind. He was almost certain the redhead had given the other girl's mind a thorough going-over, and she never seemed to make mistakes when she probed a person's mind. He remembered the odd little pause and the momentary brightness of her eyes before Philippa had given the name of her homeland. If she had lied about that, perhaps Dr. W.'s suspicions of her connection with the Circle of Life were true after all.

Even as he was thinking about her, the lady was making her way toward him, looking dazzling in a lavender skirt and a peek-a-boo shirtwaist with almost two inches of female epidermis showing below the nape of the neck through embroidered perforations. Her hair was coiled in one of the newly popular psyche knots, leaving exposed the delicate little ears and the flawless oval of her lovely face. Somehow all of Dr. W.'s accusations and the suspicions that had been forming in Dylan's own mind faded into insignificance in the presence of the lady herself.

"Ah, here you are, Mr. MacBride, hiding behind the potted plants when I had expected you to be my stellar attraction. I asked you here to be lionized and find you hiding like a shy little boy."

"I'm afraid I'm a bit intimidated by the brilliance of your guests," Dylan said. "I am not equal to the high level of philosophical discussion and transcendental mysteries of such fine minds."

"Oh, pooh!" Lady Philippa said. "I'm sure your mind is a good as any here, and how many of them actually saw the fearful Kar Kaballa himself?"

How did she know that? Dylan wondered. It was not generally known that he had twice confronted the leader of the Gogs in his own land, any more than it was common knowledge that he and Clarinda, with the help of a few friends, had destroyed the primal being Cythraul that the Gogs worshiped.

"Is it true that you and Miss MacTague had something to do with the annihilation of the being who created and controlled the Gogs?"

Without letting his surprise show, Dylan said, "We had some small part in it."

"How fascinating! I had hoped Miss MacTague would come with you. I've heard so much about her religion. The outré and the exotic in the field of mysticism always intrigue me. She must be what my friends call an 'old soul.' "

Dylan's eyebrows lifted in polite inquiry. "I don't believe I understand that term."

"Then come and meet two people I know who are old souls, Angel Annie and her guru, Master Koot Hoomi. Annie is our resident mystic and has extraordinary powers and wisdom gained from tapping the ultimate source of all knowledge."

"And what exactly would that be?" Dylan asked as he followed the girl across the room toward a tall, enormously fat woman in a purple robe.

Lady Philippa didn't answer his question, but said excitedly, "You'll feel her power as soon as you speak to her."

"Annie, this is Mr. Dylan MacBride, who rescued me yesterday when my horse ran away."

The woman turned to look at Dylan. Her multiple chins quivered and a few strands of violet hair pulled loose from the careless pile on top of her head. There was a wart on the end of her nose and her black button eyes were almost buried in the rolls of fat above her heavily rouged cheeks.

"Ah, yes, the explorer, the one who would explore the Ice Caves of Issapon," she said in a near bellow. "My advice to you, young sir, is to go quickly on your voyage or the opportunity may be lost forever."

"Really?" Dylan said. "How would you know that?"

"We who have the power know many things," Angel Annie

rumbled. "We know that which is hidden and that which is yet to be."

Bilge! Clarinda's voice said in his mind. *She's as devoid of the power as a Druidic novitiate. But watch the other one, the little dark boyo, Koot Whatchamacallit. There's something about him that gives me the shivers in me innards.*

Someone else came up to be presented to Angel Annie and Lady Philippa drew Dylan in the direction of a short, dark-skinned round-faced young man. She whispered to Dylan that although Master Koot Hoomi looked to be in his early twenties, he was in reality several hundred years old.

"It is with pleasure that I meet you, sir," Koot Hoomi said. "I sense that you are a person who has seen strange sights and done important things, that even now you are preparing for an adventure of deep interest."

"Yes, I have been making plans for an expedition to Issapon to explore the Ice Caves," Dylan said, and then added, "but another matter has come up unexpectedly which may mean a cancellation or postponement of my project."

A frown creased the placid brow of Koot Hoomi. "That would be a mistake. Nothing must keep you from your destiny. I can see what fame your discoveries will bring you, what honors will be conferred upon you for unlocking the secrets of that far place. You will astonish the world with the knowledge you bring back to civilization. Your findings will have great mystical significance as well as economic value."

"Mystical and economic," Dylan repeated. Somebody, it seemed, wanted very badly for him to speed his departure from Avallon. "I don't understand what you mean, sir."

A flicker of irritation showed in the burning eyes for the briefest of seconds. "I mean that in the Ice Caves you may find evidence not only of man's origins but of his ultimate fate as well. If the sight that is given me is not mistaken, you will find clues of a civilization so ancient that it had crumbled before Emrys of the Hundred Towers was raised."

"That would be exciting, of course, but—"

"And you will find treasure beyond belief," the master continued quickly. "Treasure that will make the Golconda seem like nothing."

Yes, they wanted him out of the way, Dylan thought, and if promised discoveries weren't enough to do the job, they'd promise him treasure. Why? What was behind these glowing predictions of success?

The master passed a hand before his eyes. "There is one more vision, but I can see it only dimly . . . a craft . . . some kind of iron vessel you will need on your mission. The name is unclear—wait—Thunder-something. Do you know of such a craft?"

"Yes," Dylan admitted. So they not only wanted him to leave, they wanted him to go in the *Thunderbolt*. How interesting. Did they simply want to get rid of the diving ram or did they hope he would take the unstable craft on the high seas where it would be lost with all hands, without a trace?

"I strongly urge you to go as soon as possible, Mr. Mac-Bride, and to go in the one ship which can assure your success," Koot Hoomi concluded.

"Well, I certainly appreciate the trouble you've taken to look into these things for me," Dylan said.

Even white teeth showed in a smile. "It is no trouble. We who are in tune with the infinite know these things without bothering to, as you say, 'look into.' "

Lady Philippa guided Dylan over to a punch bowl where a nonalcoholic beverage was being served in keeping with the advanced view of the professor and his guests. Some of the other guests claimed the lady's attention and Dylan stood sipping at the bland concoction, wondering about Koot Hoomi. He didn't recognize the man's race or probable origin. It was possible that he didn't know all the races on the planet, of course, but on the other hand, Angel Annie and Koot Hoomi spoke Anglic with the same slight accent that Lady Philippa and her uncle did. Could it be that they were all from Earth and all members of the Circle of Life? If so, then they might suspect that he had been contacted by Dr. W. and would be working to circumvent any action he might take.

Suddenly he became aware of Koot Hoomi's luminous brown eyes fixed on him from across the room, staring so intently that it almost seemed as though the guru was trying to look into his soul.

Not your soul, me bucko. He's been tryin' to probe your mind. I ran into his muckin' about in here a few minutes ago and ran him out. He had no business doin' that.

There's some other people who haven't got any business

muckin' about in my mind either! Dylan said, irritated at the way she kept slipping in and out without his detecting her presence until she chose to reveal it.

Well, I never! And me just tryin' to help! Clarinda said and was gone with an almost audible swish of her skirt.

Dylan felt a small pang of regret but at least he wouldn't have to worry about her overhearing any of his conversations for the remainder of the evening. And when the party was over and he was taking leave of his host and hostess, it was just as well that the redhead wasn't around.

"We do hope you won't be a stranger from now on, Mr. MacBride," Lady Philippa murmured, squeezing his hand as he bent to kiss her fingertips.

"Drop in any time, my boy," Professor Philander urged. He was a short, balding man with a white goatee and a mild, almost vague manner. He turned to go back into the house but paused to smile and observe, "My niece and I feel that we have known you in a previous life."

Dylan's eyes widened and he looked quickly at Lady Philippa as her uncle wandered off.

"Yes, Dylan—and I'm going to presume on our former acquaintance and use your first name—what he says is true. I have been remembering details of our past lives all evening."

"You astonish me," Dylan said. "I wasn't aware that I had lived before."

"Lived and loved before, Dylan," she said with a faint blush and a flutter of long dark lashes.

"I'm afraid I'm not in the least psychic, Lady Philippa," Dylan said hastily. "I remember nothing of any past life. In fact, sometimes I have trouble remembering what I've done in this one."

His weak attempt at levity didn't please Lady Philippa. Her large limpid eyes misted over and she gazed at him reproachfully but lovingly. "Don't you see, Dylan, we were destined to meet along the Strand. It has been our fate since the beginning of time to be reunited in the next life after having been separated by death in the previous one."

"Uh . . . well . . . I certainly have enjoyed the evening," Dylan said. "I'll just hail a hansom and be on my way."

"Not until you promise to come back to see me," she said, clinging to his hand. "I couldn't bear it if I thought we were going to be parted for a long period again."

"Yes, of course, I'll come by again," Dylan said, withdrawing his hand as gently as possible and backing down the steps. "Good night, Lady Philippa, and thank you for inviting me."

Finding a hansom was easier said than done. The fog was drifting in again, and there was only one rig visible on the street. It was sitting some thirty feet away under a street lamp, and the hackman was the same tall, thin, oddly dressed man who had driven him here. It was too much of a coincidence. The fellow must be up to something, Dylan thought and decided he'd rather walk.

Gripping his cane firmly in his hand, he started down the street toward the mass of greenery that marked Paradise Gardens. He'd cut through the park and catch an omnibus on South Park Drive and be home in half an hour.

"Cab, sir?" the lanky man called as Dylan hurried off. "Wouldn't you be wanting a cab, mister?"

Dylan pretended not to hear and in a few minutes was passing through the gates of the park, going past the amusement center which was closed for the night and entering the more densely wooded central area.

Once he thought he heard a footfall behind him but when he turned to look there were only shadows and drifting fog. He had the uneasy feeling that he was being watched or followed.

Clarinda? Are you there, Clarinda? He formed the words in his mind, trying to reach out to her, but there was no answer. She must be really furious with him.

With nothing but the echo of his own footsteps to keep him company, Dylan followed the path beneath the overhanging trees. It was dark and the drifting swirls of fog didn't help any in finding the way. He had just gone down into a little vale, a sunny play area for children in the daytime but chilly and vaguely menacing now, and was beginning to wonder if he hadn't made a mistake in cutting through the park when something appeared on the path ahead that made him certain he had.

"My God, what is *that*?" he gasped, staring at the great striped animal with glittering yellow eyes, bared fangs and lashing tail. He had never seen a beast like it in his life although it did bear a faint resemblance to the large cat creatures on the continent of Uffern.

Whatever it was, he knew it was about to attack him from

the way it was crouched down on its hind legs, tensed to leap. Flight would be hopeless. He could only stand and face what must surely be certain death, but he resolved to sell his life as dearly as possible. He gripped his stout cane and watched the beast's eyes, hoping to gauge the precise second when it would leap so he might have some small chance of moving to the side and striking as it pounced.

"Keridwen, great lady, say goodbye to Clarinda for me." The words were almost like a prayer as the great creature hurled itself through the air at him.

"Don't move, sir," said a gruff voice behind him, and there was a loud report from a heavy weapon.

Hit between the eyes, the beast fell thrashing at Dylan's feet. He stared down at the dead animal in shock and relief and then turned to face his rescuer.

"A very near thing, Mr. MacBride, a very near thing," said the mysterious hackman, coming from behind a tree holding an enormous horse pistol in one hand. "You're a lucky man. Lucky that I was nearby and that I carry this gun. There's precious few pistols would stop a thing like that. Lucky also that I am the surest shot you're likely to find."

And so modest, Dylan thought, but aloud he said, "Thank you for saving my life. What is that beast?"

"Why, a tiger, of course," the bewhiskered one said. "Never seen one, eh? No, I don't suppose you would, since there's no area on this world that corresponds to the Indian subcontinent where the beasts originate on Earth."

"Earth again," Dylan said. "See here, just exactly who are you?"

The hackman pulled at his chin whiskers and smiled through the lush foliage. "Well, there's some who say I'm one thing and some who say I'm another," he said, putting the horse pistol out of sight under the cape of his greatcoat.

But Dylan suddenly lost interest in the man's identity as the dead tiger lying at his feet vanished as quickly as it had appeared in front of him. "It's gone! By Keridwen's snow-white bosom, how can that be?"

"I suspect because it was a were-tiger," the cabman said. "I fancy such things are not a regular part of the entertainment in Paradise Gardens, are they, sir?"

"A were-tiger? No, hardly," Dylan said, examining the spot where the creature had fallen.

"I thought not. No more than a were-tiger would even be

possible on my world. I suspect the natural laws are different here on Annwn."

"I still don't understand where such a beast would come from," Dylan said.

"I'll bid you good night, sir. I have work to do and you're perfectly safe now, I imagine, since conjuring up one of those things takes an uncommon amount of work and our friend Koot Hoomi is probably sleeping it off right now."

"Are you trying to tell me that—"

"Good night, sir," the man said. "I have to resume my surveillance of the Philander house. If you should happen on Dr. W., you might tell him that an old friend from back home sends his good wishes."

The man disappeared into the fog-filled shadows, leaving Dylan muttering to himself. Back home? Earth? There were getting to be as many people from that once-mythical place wandering around Avallon as there were natives.

And why should Koot Hoomi want to kill him? Assuming, of course, that the little dark man had the power to materialize a beast like that. First two people thought to be members of the Circle of Life had tried to get him to leave Avallon and then one of them had tried a more direct method of removing him from the scene. Did he represent a menace to their plans just by being in the city? Why him rather than Dr. W. or the mysterious hackman?

With thoughts like these rioting through his mind, Dylan hurried through Paradise Gardens to the gate that opened onto South Park Lane. The street was brightly lit by the new electric lights which were coming more and more into use in the city, and their glow was a welcome relief after the darkness of the park. It was only a few minutes until a wheezing, puffing steam omnibus came braking to a stop. Dylan climbed aboard, deposited his three-penny fare and was on his way home.

Chapter 5

Dylan had just sat down to breakfast when the wire began rattling. With a regretful glance at the perfectly poached and delicious kippers Mrs. Vanders had prepared for him, he crossed the room to pick up the speaking tube.

"Is it that this is Mr. Dylan MacBride?" Professor Lombosa asked.

"This is MacBride," Dylan said. "What is it?"

"I have news of most startling and significant importance. The mighty ironclad diving ram is again in repair and ready for her trials."

"She was lying on a mud bank only three days ago," Dylan said. "How can she have been repaired so quickly?"

"It was merely a matter of balance," Lombosa said. "Since we have lightened the craft, she rides high and safe in the water, is it not so?"

"You lightened her balance and solved all the problems?" Dylan said skeptically. "I find that hard to believe."

"But is it not so that Lombosa is a genius?" the Bellicosan inventor asked.

Dylan didn't answer that. Instead he asked, "How about the weak engines?"

"Well, that minor detail is perhaps not so solved as the other," Lombosa admitted. "But with the vessel in a lighter condition, the engines will propel her faster, is it not that you think?"

Dylan felt that Bellicosan must be a very difficult language to learn considering what Lombosa did to Anglic.

"What have you done about the leaking hatch covers and ventilators?"

"They are now covered with tarpaulin and most excellently waterproofed," Lombosa said.

It seemed to Dylan that waterproof canvas was not enough to keep out the tons of water that had poured into

49

the *Thunderbolt,* but perhaps with a higher freeboard it might work. And since Dr. W. had been interested in the craft as a possible weapon against the Circle of Life's hidden colony, it might be best if he took another look at it.

"When are you going to take her out?" he asked.

"This very morning," Lombosa said. "It is too important that it be perfected for it to wait."

"Very well. I'll ride out there after breakfast," Dylan said and hung up the speaking tube.

Before he could sit down at the table, there was a loud knocking on the garden door and he opened it to find a freckle-faced, redheaded boy of about twelve standing there. It was one of Clarinda's younger brothers but for the life of him, Dylan couldn't remember if it was Paddy, Shawn, Mike or Terrence.

"Me sister says you are not to go in that iron sinkin' boat," the boy said. "She says the next time it sinks, it'll take you right down with it."

Dylan stared at the child in surprise. "Why the messenger service? Your sister usually delivers her own messages right into my head."

"She sent me 'cause she's not talkin' to the likes of you," the boy said. "She also said you was to tip me a shillin' for me trouble."

Dylan had his doubts about that but he dug into his sporran and came up with sixpence which he tossed into the youngster's open palm. "Thank you, Paddy."

"You're welcome but me name is Mike," the boy said with a gap-toothed grin before he took off, scaling the garden wall like a monkey.

Dylan went back to his breakfast and was just finishing it when the front doorbell rang and the maid ushered in Major Churchward and Dr. W., who looked almost as excited as Lombosa had sounded.

"We have news," the doctor announced. "My colleague followed Koot Hoomi from the Philander house to his digs in Belham Row. And with that one in town, the rest of the rascals are not likely to be far away."

"I could have told you the gentleman was in Avallon if you'd asked me," Dylan said. "I met him at Professor Philander's soiree."

"Indeed?" Dr. W. asked. "And were you told what he was? Koot Hoomi is said to be one of the so-called Secret

Masters, a group of Tibetan supermen who have decreed that mankind should die rather than resist the second coming of the Martians. He claims to be hundreds of years old, although I think we can take that with a grain of salt, and my colleague believes him to be the most dangerous of the lot."

In view of his experience with the were-tiger, Dylan was willing to believe that.

"By the way, Doctor, I have a message for you. A tall, bewhiskered hackman said to tell you a friend from back home sends his regards."

"Eh? What? Bewhiskered hackman? Oh. Ha, ha!" the doctor seemed amused. "So that's his current disguise, is it?"

"What about your plan?" Churchward asked. "Are we still going to search Koot Hoomi's place?"

"Yes, yes, of course," Dr. W. said and then explained to Dylan: "We'd like your help, MacBride. Koot Hoomi will be away from his digs for several hours. While my colleague keeps an eye on him, we are going to search his apartment. If we can learn anything about the hidden colony from his papers, we might have a chance of nipping the Martian invasion in the bud."

Dylan could see the logic of that, although he wasn't sure of the propriety of three gentlemen searching the rooms of another while he was absent from the premises. But, he reminded himself, Koot Hoomi was not a gentleman but the presumed enemy, so such action would be proper under the circumstances.

"Are you armed, Mr. MacBride?" the doctor asked as Dylan picked up his hat and cane.

"Why, no," Dylan said, looking down at his kilts and sporran. "Do I look as though I am?"

"No, but I suggest that become so. Major Churchward and I both have our service revolvers."

Dylan nodded and went to get the thirty-eight Webley he had carried during the Goggish invasion. There wasn't room for it in his sporran, which was the only pocket available in kilts, so he had to put on a topcoat. Feeling rather melodramatic, he slipped the gun and an extra box of cartridges into the coat pocket and was ready to go.

The guru's rooms were on the second floor of a fashionable Belham Row house. To avoid passing the windows of the landlady on the first floor, the three gentlemen ascended the steps at the rear and made their way to the door of Koot Hoomi's apartment.

"Now what do we do?" Dylan asked. "I'm afraid my housebreaking training has been neglected."

"Allow me," Dr. W. said, taking a key from his pocket and inserting it in the lock. "My colleague managed to make an impression of the master's key while pretending to help him retrieve his umbrella yesterday."

Churchward laughed. "I didn't know your friend was a second-story man back on Earth. Or was his profession safe-cracking?"

"It wasn't, but if it had been, he would have been the most proficient one of all," Dr. W. said proudly and threw open the apartment door.

The rooms seemed quite ordinary. There was nothing to mark them as different from hundreds of other furnished flats in the city. In fact, they hardly gave the impression of having been lived in at all.

"Most extraordinary," the doctor said, opening the drawers of a chiffonier and finding them empty. "Our secret master doesn't even bring along a change of underwear when he travels, or a handkerchief to wipe his nose."

"Perhaps such ethereal beings don't need to change clothes or wipe their noses," Dylan said, opening the wardrobe and finding nothing but a pair of house slippers. "There is no outer apparel here either."

"Very strange," Dr. W. said. "It's almost as though the fellow wasn't really living here, and yet H. says he is and H. is never wrong."

"There are no papers in the desk," Churchward said, searching through drawers and compartments of an unlocked rolltop.

Dr. W. frowned. "Well, it doesn't seem that we are going to find any clues to the hidden colony here."

"In fact, gentlemen," a voice said from behind them. "It is possible that you will never find anything again, because here you die!"

Dylan whirled with his hand in his coat pocket. The other two stood transfixed by surprise, staring at Koot Hoomi advancing on them with scimitar in one hand and knife in the other.

Dylan didn't have time to remove the revolver from his pocket but he did have time to get his finger on the trigger and pull it. The thirty-eight blasted the stillness of the room, and Koot Hoomi, struck at point-blank range by two heavy-caliber, soft-nosed shells, dropped his weapons and crumpled.

The two Terrans and Dylan stood silently, watching the pool of blood beginning to form under the dark young man. Then in the blink of an eye there was nothing—no body, no weapons, no blood.

"Oh, I say, what frightful cheek," Dr. W. exclaimed. "The fellow didn't even have the decency to stay dead."

"Now how the devil did he do that?" Churchward said, looking at the still smoking revolver Dylan had removed from his pocket.

"Gentlemen, I suggest we get out of here fast," Dylan said, making for the door. "The landlady probably called a constable as soon as she heard the shots."

"There's a question I would like to ask, Doctor," Churchward said as they descended the stairs with due caution.

"What's that?"

"You said your colleague would be watching Koot Hoomi while we searched his digs. Why did he let the man give him the slip and surprise us that way?"

"No one . . . positively no one on either world could give H. the slip," the doctor said, tugging at his walrus mustache.

A constable was pounding his billy club on the curb as they came out onto the street, and a mounted policeman was galloping toward him. Neither officer paid the least attention to the three well-dressed gentlemen leaving the scene of a suspected crime.

"I guess it's just as well that fellow took his body off that way," Churchward said. "Now we don't have to explain it."

"I wonder if it really was a body," Dylan said.

"With two thirty-eight slugs in him it had to be a body," Dr. W. said, "and I saw the holes in him with my own eyes."

"A man who can remove his body from the scene of his death would have no trouble removing two bullets from his belly," Dylan said. "I really would like to know how your friend H. lost him in the first place."

"Why don't you ask him?" the doctor said. "That's him waiting for us at the corner, I fancy."

Dylan looked at a solemn-faced individual with mutton-chop whiskers, a flat hat, black frock coat and turned collar. He held a Bible in one hand and an umbrella in the other.

"Then the hackman I met wasn't H?"

"No, you were right! He was the hackman and now he is this Reformed Anglic priest," Dr. W. said. "Tomorrow he may be a little old lady in a shawl on her way to the greengrocer, or the spiv in a pin-striped suit off to see his ladylove. An expert at disguise as well as all the other arms of detection is our Mr. H."

"He also wrote *the* book on surveillance," Dylan said dryly, "but apparently Koot Hoomi didn't read it."

"All will be explained in good time," the doctor said as they came closer to the man in the garb of a high church minister.

"I gather there was a disturbance at Koot Hoomi's rooms," Mr. H. said when they were within speaking distance, "and at least two shots were fired."

"Extraordinary, H." Dr. W. said admiringly.

"Elementary, my dear W." Mr. H. said. "Mr. MacBride has powder burns at two bullet holes in his coat."

"Ask him what happened to the two bullets that made those holes," Dylan said.

Mr. H. looked at him inquiringly. "Should I know?"

"Well, the last time we saw them they were in the body of Master Koot Hoomi. They disappeared along with him from his rooms after he attacked us."

"We thought you were watching him, H." Dr. W. said a little reproachfully.

"I was and I am. If you will look, you can see the gentleman in question sitting near the front window of the restaurant across the street. If I am not mistaken, he is lunching on ravioli with clam sauce accompanied by a bottle of Zinfandel of excellent aroma and bouquet but with a slight accent of vinegary acetifaction."

They took turns looking. It was unmistakably the same little dark man who had attacked them.

"Clam sauce on ravioli," Dr. W. said with a shudder. "Barbarous!"

"This is impossible," Churchward said. "The man is dead. Dead men don't eat ravioli and drink Zinfandel of whatever aroma or accent."

"I believe you gentlemen are telling me that Koot Hoomi appeared in his rooms while you were there, attacked you—"

"With scimitar and knife," Churchward said.

"—and Mr. MacBride shot him twice."

"Yes," Churchward said, "and with heavy-caliber bullets."

"But if he was never out of your sight, H., he couldn't have been in that room. It is impossible," Dr. W. said.

"Improbable but not impossible, my dear W.," Mr. H. said. "In the short time I have been on this planet, I have deduced that its natural laws are different from what we are used to. Koot Hoomi, who was a fraud on our Earth, has real powers on this world. It also explains something else that I couldn't account for at the time. You see, about fifteen minutes ago, I saw our man suddenly jerk twice and clutch at his middle. I assumed he was experiencing a gas pain or an attack of indigestion, but now I know the truth of it."

"Then perhaps you could enlighten us," Dylan said.

"Astral projection is the only possible explanation," H. said. "Koot Hoomi is apparently capable of projecting his astral body over considerable distances, and when his astral body was struck by your bullets, he felt the pain."

"Then why isn't he leaking Zinfandel from the two holes?" Churchward asked.

"Because his astral body was hit, not his real one. His real body felt the pain but is undamaged. He probably leaves his astral body on guard at the apartment at all times."

"On guard against what? There wasn't anything there," Churchward said. "No clothes, no papers, nothing."

H.'s eyes took on a brighter light. "Perhaps a closer observation might turn something up. I believe I'll have a look myself."

"But the police are there now," the doctor objected.

"And they will think it perfectly natural for a man of the cloth to show up at the scene of possible violence to comfort and advise," H. pointed out. "So if you gentlemen will take over my duty of watching the subject, I shall go offer my services to those who may need them."

"How long should we keep Koot Hoomi under observation?" Churchward asked.

Mr. H. drew from his pocket a large watch of the kind clergymen favored. "For approximately forty-five minutes more. At that time he has a reservation in a reading room of the Imperial Service Museum that he won't risk losing. He will be there for the rest of the afternoon."

Dylan was puzzled. "What an odd place for a mystic to

go."

"He is studying the military tactics of the Avallonian forces in depth," Mr. H. said. "He is doing it for the benefit of his Martian friends."

He hurried off, leaving them to make what they would of that.

Exactly forty minutes later, Koot Hoomi rose from his table, paid the check and walked toward the Imperial Services Museum three blocks away. Dylan followed him at a discreet distance but reached the lobby in time to see him present his reservation at the desk and be escorted to a reading room where a cartful of books on military subjects was rolled in by a page. Dylan then returned to where he had left the others and found that Mr. H. had rejoined them.

"I assume you found nothing more than we did," Dylan said.

"You assume wrong, young fellow. I found a great deal. If all else fails, it may be enough to lead us to the hidden colony."

"But we didn't see anything like that."

"Did you just look or did you really scrutinize? What I found was a leaf from the *Mimusops huberi*, commonly called the Brazilian cowtree or massarandriba, plus some mud from a carboniferous bed of the sort usually exposed in the basin of the Amazon River, plus a tiny fragment of yareta or azoreila, a mosslike cushion plant of the carrot family which the natives of the upper Amazon use for fuel. The leaf was on the floor under the bed, the mud had been scraped off on the doormat as had also the azoreila."

Dylan was impressed but also mystified. "Do you mean that the colony is in a place called the Amazon River valley? I'm an explorer and I've never heard of such a place."

"And for a very good reason," H. said. "It is on our world, not yours. I was not saying that's where the colony is, only that it's in an area which generally corresponds to the Amazon River basin with its swampy meadows, its rain forests and mangrove thickets. Is there such a place on this planet? On this continent?"

"Well, yes, there are the great rain forests of Tir-Narog and Broccliande, and the Myrk River basin runs through them out beyond the Prefecture of the West."

"Ah, I thought as much. So if we can get no better information, we shall have to search the banks of the Myrk River for the location of this mud and this leaf."

"That really is an extraordinary talent you have," Dylan said.

"Elementary, my dear MacBride, to the trained eye and analytical mind. However, we need more evidence so we can pinpoint the exact location. Time is now of the essence."

The urgency in his voice caused the other three to exchange uneasy glances. "I say, H.," Dr. W. said, "are you holding out on us? Have you information you haven't told us?"

"Nothing that isn't common knowledge," H. said, handing Dylan a copy of the latest edition of the Avallon *Express*. "There's a short item on page seven that you might share with the good doctor and Major Churchward."

Dylan folded the paper to page seven and found the item. " 'Mysterious blasts on planet Thor,' " he read with rising excitement. " 'Scientists at the observatory at Emrys of the Hundred Towers, located 1,500 miles to the northwest of Avallon, reported seeing a series of six blasts on the surface of the planet Thor. Another astronomer hundreds of miles away confirmed the report and added that there were six more blasts on the following night.' "

"They are coming, gentlemen," Mr. H. said. "The second Martian invasion is on its way."

Chapter 6

Dylan entered his apartment to hear the wire rattling loudly. He picked up the tube and spoke into it.

"Dylan, thank the gods!" It was Noel Bran ap Lynn. "We thought you were dead! The O'Haras and I have been frantic!"

"Dead? I don't understand. I assure you I am quite well."

"Alice called to invite you to their second anniversary party and was told by the maid that you had gone on that damn ironclad ram."

"The *Thunderbolt?*" Dylan said. He had completely forgotten his appointment with Lombosa when Churchward and Dr. W. had arrived and asked him to accompany them to Koot Hoomi's rooms. "Yes, I was scheduled to go along on another trial run this morning."

"Thank the gods you didn't!" Noel said. "The damn thing sank in Lake Regillos with all hands . . . all except that Lombosa fellow."

"Keridwen!" Dylan said, a cold spot forming in the pit of his stomach. It was the merest coincidence that he hadn't been aboard the ram. He hated to admit it, but Clarinda had been right.

"Noel, something else has come up that I think you should know about. Would it be possible for you and O'Hara and a few other fellows with a concern for the welfare of the country to meet with Major Churchward and myself soon? We've come on something pretty frightening and I feel some action should be taken."

"Why not at the O'Haras' party?"

"No, I think not. An anniversary celebration isn't the place for a discussion of this kind."

"You really are serious, aren't you?" Noel asked. "All right, how would tomorrow afternoon do, at the United Service Club, say? I'll get in touch with St. John and van Rasselway and you bring Churchward."

"Fine," Dylan said, "and there will also be two other gentlemen from Earth."

"Earth again, is it? I don't know what we're going to do with all these immigrants."

"I think we have some potential immigrants from even further away to worry about," Dylan said.

"Further away than Earth? You haven't been looking into Clarinda's crystal ball, have you, old boy?"

"You might say that. I'll fill you in on it all when I see you tomorrow," Dylan said.

He had no sooner hung up than a scratching came at the garden door. When he opened it, there was a redheaded, freckle-faced boy scowling at him.

"Come in, Shawn," Dylan invited.

"I'm Paddy, not Shawn, and I can say me piece standin' right here."

"Fine," Dylan said, smiling. "Say away."

"Me sister says to tell you that she told you so but you wouldn't listen and would have gone off in that iron sinkin' boat if you hadn't got yourself mixed up in that other mess with that guru fella. She says it was just blind, dumb luck that you didn't get killed twice over and next time you better listen to her divine guidance."

"Tell your sister I said thanks for wanting to save my life even it I didn't pay any attention to her and managed to stay alive anyway."

"She also says you should give me two shillin's for remindin' you of her all-seein', all-knowin' power, and for remindin' you to keep your Sassenach paws off that Earth woman or see her turn into a snake in your embrace."

Dylan laughed. "Paddy, I want you to go back and tell your beautiful but uppity sister that if she's too good to deliver her own messages, she can darn well mind her own business."

"Oh, I'd niver dare!" Paddy said. "She's doin' the washin' and she'd be like to duck me in the tub if I delivered any such cheeky message."

"Here's sixpence," Dylan said, handing him a coin. "Now run along and tell her what I told you to."

The lad looked at the coin in disgust. "Shawn said all you Vinelanders was penny-squeezers."

"You'd better get out of here before I . . ." Dylan aimed a half-serious kick at the boy's posterior, and Paddy streaked across the garden and up over the wall.

Dylan shut the door, poured himself a drink and settled down for an evening of serious reading with H. G. Wells's historical account of the *War of the Worlds.*

The next afternoon Major Churchward, Dr. W. and Mr. H. accompanied Dylan to the United Service Club for the meeting with Noel and his friends. In addition to O'Hara, St. John and van Rasselway, Dylan was surprised to find that the aged General Horwitz had come along. Over whiskey and soda, the military group was told of the existence and menace of the Martians.

"Martians?" was Noel's first reaction. "That's even more fantastic than Gogs!"

"Well, the Gogs were very real, if you remember," Dylan said.

"Yes, but at least they had been heard of on Annwn.

What do you suppose would happen if we tried to convince people of the existence of a race of beings called Martians who come from a planet they've never heard of and can't see because it's in another dimension?"

"The invasion is coming from Thor, not Mars," Dylan said. "We continue to call the creatures Martians because it is convenient. What would you call an inhabitant of Thor, a Thorian?"

"All I'm saying is that we had a devil of a time convincing the higher echelons of the reality of a Goggish invasion, so you can see how hard this will be," Noel said.

"Of course, reports are coming into the Astronomical Exchange from observatories all over the world relating to the unexpected activity on Thor's usually quiet surface," St. John said thoughtfully. "I've been wondering what was causing the explosions myself."

"Tell me about their weapons," General Horwitz said. "What do you know about the fire-shooting thing and the smoke?"

"Not too much," Mr. H. said. "Their technology is far in advance of ours and that makes their weapons vastly superior. Shortly after the first capsule landed and opened, they produced a gadget which looked like a camera, but it could project a ray of heat thousands of yards. If we had known of these ahead of time, perhaps something could have been done before the capsule opened or immediately afterward. If guns had been brought up and had started firing the moment the hatches were raised, before they had time to set up the heat-rays, the invasion might have been nipped in the bud."

"Or if you had dynamited the thing when it first landed or during its cooling-off period," Churchward suggested.

"Hindsight is always better than foresight," Dr. W. observed a little testily. "That is why we came to warn Annwn. There is no doubt that if we had promptly executed strong countermeasures at each landing, the Martians would never have been able to get their heat-rays into action or build their battle machines. But once they had established their mobility, it became impossible to stop them."

"Several times masked batteries were able to take them by surprise, especially at river crossings and the like, and destroy individual machines," H. said. "It was then that they began to use the poisonous smoke to clear the way.

They would simply lay down a screen of thick black smoke which clung to the ground and rolled into hollows and down behind embankments where guns might be hidden, killing the men at the guns before they could open fire. There was one time, however, when the smoke didn't work. Mr. Wells describes it quite vividly in his history since his brother seems to have been an eyewitness aboard a steamer. It happened when the fleet carrying thousands of refugees fleeing England via the Thames estuary was standing out to sea and the Martians appeared in pursuit."

Dr. W. had picked up one of the copies of Wells's book they had brought with them and was flipping through it. "Yes, here's the start of that incident. I'll read you a little of it: 'A Martian appeared, small and faint in the remote distance, advancing along the muddy coast from the direction of Foulness. Every soul aboard stood at the bulwarks or on the seats of the steamer and stared at the distant shape, higher than the trees or church toward inland, and advancing with a leisurely parody of a human stride.

"'It was the first Martian my brother had seen, and he stood, more amazed than terrified, watching this Titan advancing deliberately toward the shipping, wading farther and farther into the water as the coast fell away. Then, far away beyond the Crouch, came another, striding over some stunted trees, and then yet another still farther off, wading deeply through a shiny mudflat that seemed to hang halfway up between sea and sky. They were all stalking seaward as though to intercept the escape of the multitudinous vessels that were crowded between Foulness and the Maze. . . .'"

The doctor skipped a page or two, then continued:

"'Glancing northwestward, my brother saw the large crescent of shipping already writhing with the approaching terror; one ship passing behind another, another coming round from broadside to end on, steamships whistling and giving off volumes of steam, sails being let out, launches rushing hither and thither. He was so fascinated by this and by the creeping danger away to the left that he had no eyes for anything seaward. And then a swift movement of the steamboat (she had suddenly come round to avoid being run down) flung him headlong from the seat upon which he was standing. There was a shouting all about him, a trampling of feet, and a cheer that seemed to be answered faintly. The steamboat lurched and rolled him over upon his hands.

"He sprang to his feet and saw to starboard, and not a hundred yards from their heeling, pitching boat, a vast iron bulk like the blade of a plough tearing through the water, tossing it on either side in huge waves of foam that leaped toward the steamer, flinging her paddles helplessly in the air, and then sucking her deck down almost to the waterline. . . . Big iron upperworks rose out of this head-long structure, and from that twin funnels projected and spat a smoking blast shot with fire. It was the torpedo ram, *Thunder Child*, steaming headlong, coming to the rescue of the threatened shipping.' "

Dr. W. looked up from the book and straight at Dylan. "Does that suggest something to you, Mr. MacBride?"

"I find the account very interesting, Doctor. Please continue."

"Yes, W.," H. said, "let the facts speak for themselves."

The doctor nodded and started to read again. " 'My brother looked past this charging leviathan at the Martians again, and he saw the three of them now close together, and standing so far out to sea that their tripod supports were almost entirely submerged. . . . It seemed they were regarding this new antagonist with astonishment. To their intelligence, it may be, the giant was even such another as themselves. The *Thunder Child* fired no gun, but simply drove full speed toward them.

" 'Suddenly the foremost Martian lowered his tube and discharged a canister of the black gas at the ironclad. It hit her larboard side and glanced off in an inky jet that rolled away to seaward, an unfolding torrent of black smoke, from which the ironclad drove clear. To the watchers from the steamer, low in the water and with the sun in their eyes, it seemed as though she was already among the Martians.

" 'They saw the gaunt figures separating and rising out of the water as they retreated shoreward, and one of them raised the camera-like generator of the heat-ray. He held it pointing obliquely downward, and a bank of steam sprang from the water at its touch. It must have driven through the iron of the ship's side like a white-hot iron rod through paper.

" 'A flicker of flame went up through the rising steam, and then the Martian reeled and staggered. In another moment he was cut down, and a great body of water and steam shot high in the air. The guns of the *Thunder Child* sounded through the reek, going off one after the other. . . .

" 'At the sight of the Martian's collapse the captain on the bridge yelled inarticulately, and all the crowding passengers on the steamer's stern shouted together. And then they yelled again. For, surging out beyond the white tumult, drove something long and black, the flames streaming from its middle parts, its ventilators and funnels spouting fire.

" 'She was alive still; the steering gear, it seems, was intact and her engines working. She headed straight for a second Martian, and was within a hundred yards of him when the heat-ray came to bear. Then with a violent thud, a blinding flash, her decks, her funnels, leaped upward. The Martian staggered with the violence of her explosion, and in another moment the flaming wreckage, still driving forward with the impetus of its pace, had struck him and crumpled him up like a thing of cardboard.' "

"Well done, *Thunder Child!*" O'Hara said.

"Bully!" Churchward applauded, and the others around the table made various sounds of approval.

Dylan studied their faces. A few minutes before they were unconvinced, but now the reality of the written word had won them over. They understood something of the danger now and would put their minds to work on how to cope with it.

Picking up the book the doctor had put down, Dylan flipped the pages backward to another prior incident. "General Horwitz, there's also an account here of how they ambushed one of the things at a river bank."

"Hmm, masked batteries," General Horwitz said. "They could work quite well."

"But right after that the Martians withdrew and regrouped; when they attacked next it was with the black smoke to wipe out the battery crews," Dr. W. pointed out. "There was no time to think of ways to counter the poison smoke then, but there has since been talk of respirators which could be worn over the face with chemicals to screen out the deadly gas."

"Yes, something like that could probably be improvised," Dylan said. "I've noticed something else about the accounts of these two actions, the only ones in which the forces of your empire inflicted any major damage on the monsters. Wells doesn't mention it and perhaps not too much notice of it was taken at the time, but it seems to me that even though the Martians had such overwhelming power, they were not particularly brave. After the loss of only one of their number at the river, they withdrew to their base. If they had pushed ahead, they would have taken London by complete surprise and wiped out its entire population. And again, at the moment of the *Thunder Child*'s attack on those in the channel, three of them hurriedly withdrew when the ram came among them."

"You mean the bloody things have emotions just like men?" O'Hara asked. "Or at least show evidence of fear?"

"Yes, and I'm wondering if we could somehow work out a tactic to play on their fear and use it against them."

"Good enough, my dear MacBride," H. said, "but first things first. We need Professor Lombosa's driving ram. It could be even more effective than the *Thunder Child* against the Martians."

Dylan and Noel exchanged glances.

"I'm afraid that would be a little difficult," the airship officer said. "You see, the diving ram has already dived . . . right to the bottom of Lake Regillos."

"Then it must be raised at once," H. said. "Raised, repaired and made seaworthy."

"It will also need stronger engines," Dylan said. "With the ones it has, instead of rushing toward the Martians, it would probably drift away from them if they splashed water on it as they walked."

"Yes, strong engines are of prime importance, and all of this must be done quickly," H. said, leaning forward to stare intently at each man in turn, "because, gentlemen, to again quote Wells, 'And invisible to me because it was so remote and small, flying swiftly and steadily toward me across that incredible distance, drawing nearer every minute by so many thousands of miles, came the Thing they were sending us, the Thing that was to bring so much struggle and calamity and death to the earth. I never dreamed of it then as I watched; no one on earth dreamed of that unerring missile.' "

"Yes," General Horwtiz said decisively, "we must make ready with no further delay. I will do my best to convince the War Office but we must also make independent plans."

"I have an idea," Noel said. "In skimming through the book, I see no mention of the Martians being attacked from the air, either at their landing places or while on the move. Is it possible Earth has no airships?"

"None such as your *Vengeance*," H. said. "None equipped for war. Only observation balloons and such."

"Then why not attack the Martians from the air with dynamite bombs, cannon fire and rattlers?"

"Because the heat-rays have a range of thousands of yards vertically as well as horizontally."

"But if we could get above their range," van Rasselway said excitedly, "we might do some good work."

"Yes," Noel said, "and why not use all available airships as a flying squadron to transport men and guns to the sites of Martian landings?"

"Good idea," Horwitz said. "I think I have enough influence to see that all airworthy craft will be concentrated here at the capital ready to speed to the scene of any reported landing. If we can attack the things before they get out of their capsules, they may find a warned and ready Annwn a much tougher nut to crack than a surprised and unprepared Earth."

"Ah, but that's where the Circle of Life comes in," H. said. "That group and its secret colony are preparing a different kind of welcome for the inhuman invaders."

"See here," St. John said impatiently, "why can't we just detain these people? A dozen armed and resolute men could arrest all of them in the city and——"

"No, no! That would only serve to alert those already at the base," H. objected. "And it would finish any chance we might have of learning its exact location."

"But I thought you had already deduced that," Churchward said.

"No, only the general area," H. said with an annoyed flick of his eyes in the major's direction. "We can find it in time but, as I pointed out, time is of the essence. If one of those capsules hurtling toward us at such a fantastic speed lands at a protected base, the game may well be up for all of us."

"So it all comes back to determining where the Circle of Life has set up their colony," Dylan said.

"It all comes back to you, MacBride," H. said. "You and Lady Philippa."

"In what way?"

"In the eternal way of a man with a maid," H. said. "In spite of her ladyship's intellectual pretensions, she is susceptible, and you are a handsome young man."

"Are you suggesting that I do something so ungentlemanly as to trifle with the young lady's affections to get information?"

H.'s eyes bored into his. "Are you suggesting there's anything you won't do to save Annwn from the approaching terror and mankind from total destruction?"

Chapter 7

Leaving the others to talk over potential plans and tactics, Mr. H. and Dylan left the meeting together, Dylan to call on Lady Philippa and the self-styled detective to take up his search for the elusive Koot Hoomi.

"I'll have you know this goes against the grain," Dylan told the Earthman. "In addition to the fact that it is ungentlemanly, it presents a personal problem."

"You mean the beauteous Clarinda, of course, but surely she can understand that the fate of the human race is at stake."

"I'm not sure Clarinda would think the human race more important than—"

"Is that any way to talk about a lady when she's not around to defend herself?" Clarinda asked.

For a moment Dylan continued to walk along, thinking the girl was talking in his mind. Then he realized he had heard her voice with his ears and turned to find her standing a few feet away. She was dressed in what he had heard referred to as a walking costume. Her white silk blouse with leg-of-mutton sleeves was complimented by a long blue skirt with mauve bands and decorated with mauve rosettes. A matching zouave jacket accented the nipped-in waist and matched the jaunty little blue hat with its mauve feather. A parasol of the same colors completed the outfit which seemed to have been designed especially to show off her vivid coloring and voluptuous figure.

"Clarinda, what are you doing here?" Dylan asked.

"Just out takin' a bit of a stroll," she said, grinning and twirling her parasol, "and maybe takin' a peek or two in the fancy boutiques. A lady likes to keep up with the fashions, you know."

Dylan didn't know a woman who was less interested in fashion than the redheaded priestess, and if she did any shopping at all it was simply by reaching out with the power and helping herself.

"Aren't you goin' to introduce me to the distinguished gentleman from the other world?"

"Oh, of course. I'm forgetting my manners," Dylan said, wondering what she was up to. "Clarinda MacTague, may I present a friend of Major Churchward's, Mr. H."

"Mr. Aitch, faith and that's a fine name," the girl said, smiling and offering her hand to the tall, thin man who took it with a ceremonious little bow and lift of his hat as he kissed it.

"Besides being a lovely lady, Clarinda MacTague, you are in the ministry," Mr. H. said. "You have come on foot from Trogtown where your temple is located and you had to discipline a small child before leaving home."

Clarinda looked a little uneasy as she withdrew her hand. "Sure and you make a girl feel she's bein' seen right through. How would you be knowin' all them things about me?"

Mr. H. preened himself slightly. "Observation, my dear lady. Observation with an acutely trained eye."

"You mean you don't have the second sight?"

"No. I have merely trained my eyes to notice many small details and my mind to interpret them. Your shoes have a little coal dust on them that one doesn't find on the clean-swept sidewalks of the upper city. There is a faint hint of insence on your fingertips such as might be found in a temple, and one of your hands has a broken fingernail as well as being slightly red, which leads me to the conclusion that you perhaps used it on the bottom of a naughty child."

Clarinda looked at her hand, then lifted her skirt a little and peered down at her shoes, showing a very pretty ankle as she did so. "You're right," she said. "That's wonderful, absolutely wonderful."

"Elementary, my dear Miss MacTague," H. said.

"Is it now?" Clarinda said with a giggle that really didn't go with so large and striking a girl, especially one who was priestess of a fertility cult. "I'm not trained in the art of observation but let me see if I can tell a few things about you, sir."

Tilting her head to one side, she put a finger under her chin and studied Mr. H. intently. "Yes . . . I see . . . hmm, you were born in the year 1854 at a farmstead called Mycroft in the North Riding of Yorkshire, a county of a country called England. Your mother was Violet Sherrinford and your father Siger Holmes. As a young boy, you traveled extensively on the continent of Europe with your parents and brothers. You attended two colleges, Oxford and Cambridge, but didn't get a degree from either because you were more interested in various esoteric subjects than in the regular curriculum. Shortly after leaving the university, you became a consulting detective, and you and Dr. W. have rooms together on a place called Baker Street in the city of London." Clarinda had said all of this very seriously and without a trace of her usual accent, but now her expression became teasing and her voice matched it. "Ah, yes, and there's a woman! She's called Irene Adler . . . and my, my, 'tis the only lady in your life. You're a consistent one, Mr. H. I wish I could say the same for the likes of the Mac-Bride."

For a minute Dylan thought Mr. H. was going to faint. He had grown pale, his eyes bulged, and when he tried to speak, he stuttered. "I-I don't know wh-what to s-say."

"No need to say anything," Dylan said. "Most likely she's reading your thoughts."

"Now you know I never intrude," Clarinda said indignantly. "It's against me principles and the bylaws of the sisterhood."

Mr. H. had recovered himself but was still staring at Clarinda. "That is the most extraordinary display of mental telepathy I have ever been privileged to witness."

"Why, thank you kindly, sir," Clarinda said with a little curtsy. "I'd not be knowin' what this mental telepathy is but if it's anything like the *fith-fath*, the *tag hairn* or the *glamourie*, I fancy I have it."

"This is capital luck, MacBride!" Mr. H. said, clapping

Dylan on the shoulder in his enthusiasm. "This girl is the best weapon we have! She can keep an eye on the members of the Circle from a distance as well as look into their very minds."

"What Circle?" Clarinda asked suspiciously. "You don't mean them people tryin' to help the octopussies from Thor?"

"The Circle of Life is a group of people from Earth who think the Martians are a superior race; they are trying to help the Martians establish themselves on Annwn," Dylan said.

"Then I wouldn't touch their minds with a twenty-mile pole," Clarinda said. "And you'd not be askin' me to, love, if you'd had a look in those octopussies' minds like I did."

"You've seen into the minds of the Martians?" H. said. "Good Lord!"

"I touched them once but never again!" Clarinda said, shuddering. "It was like bein' inside a watch or an addin' machine."

"We're not asking you to touch the Martians' minds," Dylan said. "Only those of their Earth supporters."

"The same thing it would be," Clarinda said. "If they're willin' to help the beasties, their minds must be the same: no thoughts or feelin's just clickin' and turnin' wheels. It fair turns a girl's blood to ice, it does."

"Clarinda, this is important," Dylan pleaded. "It's so important that I've agreed to do something I'd never do under other circumstances."

"Sure now, and you've been achin' to make love to that bustle-twitchin' blackhead all the time! I've been feelin' you pullin' at the reins like an overheated stallion from the very beginnin'!"

"That isn't true," Dylan said, "and please let me finish what I was trying to say. I have been asked to do a very ungentlemanly thing, to pretend affection for the lady in order to get information from her."

"And why would you worry about it's bein' ungentlemanly? She was unladylike enough to make up that cock-and-bull story about the pair of you bein' lovers in some past life, wasn't she?"

"Oh, so you overheard that too," Dylan said grimly. "Well, how do you know it's a cock-and-bull story? Maybe we did have a relationship in the past."

Clarinda shook her head until the red curls bounced. "No,

she's lying! It's impossible, me bucko, 'cause you and I have been lovers through all time . . . ever since we were clam and shellfish in the primal mud."

"Well, this is all beside the point," Dylan said, embarrassed by the girl's frankness in front of a near stranger. "We have to find out where the secret colony of the Circle of Life is, and if you won't probe the minds of the members, I'll just have to do the best I can with her ladyship."

"That one will twist you around her little finger and make a posy of you," Clarinda warned. "And you'll have nothin' for your trouble but a case of hives and a bottom covered with boils, which is what I'm wishin' on you."

"Clarinda, please use the power."

"No, I couldn't stand their evil, tickin' minds turnin' out answers like crazy machines."

"They're not really crazy," Mr. H. pointed out.

"Not crazy to be wantin' to see mankind destroyed so a bunch of octopussies can overrun the worlds? That's crazier than crazy."

"No," H. said. "By their own lights, they are very sane indeed. They suffer merely from an excess of enlightenment, an overdose of intelligence, one might say. They are so convinced of their own superiority that they can find no worth in the general run of mankind. Consequently, when they behold beings whom they consider to be their mental superiors, they feel they must join with them in an attack on their mental inferiors. Confusing intellect with moral superiority is not an aberration confined to the members of the Circle."

"Do I sense another superior mind admirin' the invaders?" Clarinda asked sharply.

"You mistake my analytical conclusion for a moral judgment," H. said. "There is a difference, you know."

"Just because I'm the high priestess of a fertility cult, there's no need for you to be thinkin' I know nothin' of morals," Clarinda said.

"This discussion is getting us nowhere," Dylan said. "I'll go on to the professor's house and see what I can do."

"Boils and hives," Clarinda said. "Don't forget, I warned you!" And she turned on her heel and flounced away, parasol twirling angrily.

"A most remarkable young lady," Mr. H. said. "Perhaps the second most remarkable woman I have ever met."

"Certainly the most stubborn," Dylan said.

Half an hour later he was being shown into the parlor of the Philander house and greeted warmly by Lady Philippa.

"I'm so glad you came to call, Dylan," she said as he kissed her hand. "I wanted so much to see you again but was afraid I might have put you off by my frankness at our last meeting."

"Not at all," Dylan said politely, "but you certainly gave me something to think about."

She gazed soulfully into his eyes. "I felt that I had to speak. There are so few of us who remember our past lives, and in order to keep us from passing like ships in the night, I had to act in what must have seemed like a very unmaidenly manner."

"Not at all," Dylan assured her again. "The idea of having known you before is quite intriguing although I had never heard the term 'old soul' before and—"

"As old as Babylon, my friend," Lady Philippa said with a soft, intimate laugh. "We were together then, you know, when Babylon was great."

Dylan didn't know what or where Babylon was or when it had existed but he was pretty sure having been there didn't give him a pedigree nearly as long as the one Clarinda had provided by claiming they had been clam and shellfish together.

"Why don't we stroll through the garden?" Lady Philippa suggested, pressing his arm with her long white fingers. "The servants won't disturb us there."

There was something so possessive about that soft little hand that Dylan winced inwardly, remembering Clarinda's prediction that the Terran woman would twist him around her finger and make a posy of him.

But he wasn't a total fool. He was capable of telling reality from fantasy. He had never loved this woman in Babylon or anywhere else and nothing too terrible could happen on a walk through the garden.

The girl stood up and he did too, offering her his arm as he started to take a step toward the open glass doors . . . tried to take a step and fell flat on his face at Lady Philippa's feet.

"What is it, Dylan? Are you all right?" Philippa asked anxiously.

"I don't know. Perhaps a touch of vertigo," Dylan said, pushing himself to his feet and trying to step toward her only to fall again.

"What's wrong?" the girl asked in alarm.

"Nothing," Dylan said, looking at his feet, "nothing that can't be fixed, anyway. In some way I can't explain, my boot-laces seem to have gotten tied together."

"My goodness! I can't imagine how."

"I can, but it's not a fit subject to speak of in front of a lady," Dylan said, silently cursing Clarinda as he retied the laces properly and got to his feet safely.

Once in the garden, Lady Philippa led Dylan along a brick path to a small bower that was furnished with a wicker table and a bench just wide enough for two people to sit side by side as long as they didn't mind touching.

"Sit here beside me and let us watch the sun go down as we did so often in the past, Asoka, my love," she said.

"Asoka?"

"Oh, that's right, your racial memory hasn't returned yet, has it? Asoka was your name when we were young and in love in Atlantis. You've forgotten that also, haven't you?"

"I'm afraid so," Dylan said. "It's embarrassing but I don't remember a thing about it."

"You will, my darling," she said, leaning toward him with face lifted, offering him her lips. "It is destined that you will remember and love me again."

Dylan kissed the soft, warm lips apprehensively, expect-ing any second to be picked up and dumped unceremonious-ly in the fishpond or something equally outrageous.

But nothing happened as the Earth girl's lips moved and clung to his. Nothing except that he heard sobs, faint and faraway at first but becoming louder and louder until they could only be called heartbroken blubbering: Clarinda cry-ing as though her heart was shattered into a thousand pieces.

Lady Philippa pulled away from him and looked around. "What on earth is that? Where is that ghostly wailing coming from?"

"I suspect it's a banshee," Dylan said. "I've heard there's one that haunts this part of the city."

"How interesting," Philippa murmured and lifted her lips to his again.

Some time later, Dylan got to his feet and stood looking down at her. "Babylon and Atlantis, eh?"

"Babylon, Atlantis, Mu and Ur of the Chaldees," she said. Ur had a nice ancient ring to it but he doubted if it went back as far as the primal mud. Clarinda definitely had the longer claim on him, and besides, her kisses were much sweeter. "Did I have a name in this Ur place?"

"Of course. You were Ur-Nina, the founder of the first dynasty."

"A king, was I? And in Babylon?"

"There you were called Prince Cyaxeres, and I was your slave girl."

"In Atlantis?"

"I was a princess in Atlantis, and you were the high priest."

"King, prince, high priest," Dylan mused. "I certainly have come down in the world, haven't I?"

"No, and you never will, my dear," she said, standing up and pressing her slender body tight against his. "You have increased in wisdom and spirituality with each incarnation."

"Ah yes, spirituality," he said, acutely aware of the softness of her uncorseted figure molded to him. "Tell me, were we married in these other lives?"

"We never felt the need," she said. "Those whose karma is entwined need no earthly ceremonies. We didn't need them then and we don't need them now."

Dylan had a pretty good idea of what was coming next and was searching his mind for a plausible way out. What could he say that would help him avoid a case of hives and a plague of boils? What excuse could he give that wouldn't insult the lady?

"My uncle is away for the night," she whispered, "and my boudoir is right at the top of the stairs."

"I . . . you honor me beyond my wildest dreams," Dylan gulped, "but I dare not accept for the sake of your reputation."

She took his hand and began leading him gently but insistently toward the door. "We enlightened ones place no importance on earthly reputations."

"But you must," Dylan said earnestly. "Avallon, despite its size and cosmopolitan appearance, can be as gossipy as a Highland village, and once a lady's reputation is damaged by even the hint of a stain, she—"

"I tell you it doesn't matter," Philippa said, guiding him toward the stairs. "Great events in the near future will consign all such trivialities to the dustbin of history. Come, my dear, we will love as we loved in Babylon, Mu and

Atlantis, and care not a fig for the gossip of little people."

He was really in for it now. Why the devil hadn't Mr. H. assigned himself the job of getting information from this woman? He didn't have any entanglements, and certainly couldn't have a woman in the offing with the temper and power of Dylan's redheaded witch.

Philippa was leading him up the stairs, and in just a minute or two it was going to be too late.

Clarinda! Clarinda, help me! he pleaded in his mind.

Ah, go on with you! she answered at once. *You wouldn't be blarneyin' me that you're not as eager as a puppy dog to be led down the primrose path, would you?*

Clarinda, this is embarrassing. You've got to get me out of this! Dylan said as he and Philippa reached the head of the stairs.

And why would I be wantin' to do that? What kind of fertility cult priestess would I be if I tried to break up your love match with a beautiful black-haired female, even if she has got the soul of a spider?

It's not a love match and you know it! She no more loves me than I love her. She's just trying to use me.

Ah, the poor little laddie is about to be seduced into in-discretion and there's none to rescue him. Would you like me to send the fire department?

Do something!

"Come, beloved." Lady Philippa opened the door of the bedroom and drew him across the threshold.

What am I going to do?

You might try screamin', Clarinda advised. *That's what outraged virgins do in stories. 'Cept I've got ways of knowin' you don't qualify as one.*

Philippa was urging him toward a huge four-poster bed. "Once again, my love, we—"

Suddenly the early evening quiet erupted into a cacophony of sound, blasted by every noise a large city was heir to.

A fire bell clanged beneath the window and there was the heavy thump of the big horses pulling the engine. Men were shouting and police whistles blowing. A factory whistle added to the din and then there was a loud pounding on first the front door and then the rear of the Philander house.

"Open in the name of the law!" a voice shouted. "We know you're in there."

Lady Philippa's seductively lowered eyelids flew open. "What's going on?"

"It's the police," Dylan said, escaping as far as the door to the bedroom.

"Come out of there, Hackum Dan or we're comin' in to get you!" the voice yelled again over the sound of the fire bell and the heavy engines drawing closer.

"Fire! Fire!" Voices were shouting in the street as horses' hooves pounded closer and the screech of fire engine brakes echoed through the house.

"What is it? What's happening now?" Lady Philippa asked.

"I don't know but I think we had better go downstairs before the police break in or the firemen start pulling the place down about our ears."

They reached the landing on the stairs at the same moment the police broke in the back door and firemen broke in the front.

"Where is he?" the police sergeant in charge demanded. "Where's Hackum Dan?"

"Where's the fire?" the fire captain demanded as his men dragged a hose in through the parlor. "We could see the smoke from outside."

"I think you'll probably find both the fire and Hackum Dan upstairs," Dylan said. As the police and firemen headed for the stairs, he hastily kissed Lady Philippa's hand and turned to go.

"Dylan, wait—"

But he was already out the door and walking very fast toward the sidewalk. By the time he reached it, he was almost running and he could hear Clarinda's derisive laughter in his head.

Chapter 8

For the next ten days Dylan felt he was reliving the days just before Kar Kaballa and his Gogs had poured across the Ice Sea and invaded Avallon. He made the same rounds from government office to government office and in some cases even talked to the same bureaucrats, warning this time of the coming Martian invasion. Although newspaper headlines announced fresh explosions of Thor every night, no one would listen. Noel, O'Hara and General Horwitz were equally ignored.

The government had changed and yet it was the same. The Prince Regent was dead, killed near Killiwic, his head thrown over the walls of the city by the Gogs, but that hadn't resulted in more efficient rule. Emperor Michael had miraculously recovered his sanity following his son's death and had resumed the throne. The difference, however, between Emperor Michael sane and Emperor Michael insane was sometimes difficult to see. An amiable, bumbling politician from a Midland banking family served as Prime Minister and doubled as Chancellor of the Exchequer, keeping a tight rein on the treasury for the sake of his tax-paying merchant class but having little aptitude for anything else. The Dux Bellum, or Commander in Chief, was a lieutenant general whom old Horwitz had once threatened to censure for incompetency during the First Frivolk War; the two got along like stray bulldogs even yet.

The response to the warnings delivered by Dylan and his friends was not so much the mockery they had received over the Gogs, but blank stares of disbelief accompanied by curt refusals to read Wells's history. The officials would not take the simplest measures to advance the military preparedness for the event of a Martian landing.

"It almost seems as though there's someone working

against us behind the scenes," Noel said to Dylan and Sean O'Hara one early afternoon when they had paused in their fruitless traipsing from government office to government office to have a sandwich and a quick whiskey and soda at the United Service Club. "It doesn't seem possible that so many politicians could become so blindly stubborn on their own."

"There *is* someone working against us behind the scenes," Sean said. "Lady Philippa Dunnmuir."

"She is?" Dylan asked. "How?"

"Well, I found out about it when Alice, against my wishes, decided to try a little innocent flirtation to win over the always susceptible Baron Leofric. She ran into the same kind of blank wall the rest of us have. All the old roué would talk about was the beauty and intelligence of Lady Philippa and how she had explained to him the utter impossibility of there being any life on the planet Thor. The lady seems to have given him the distinct impression that she has a direct line to the Cosmic Intelligence, or some such balderdash, and had received such assurance."

"If she's going to all the trouble, she must know what we're up to," Noel said, "and if she knows, the rest of those beggars know. Gentlemen, I suggest that in the future we go armed. Those people are fanatics and as such are quite capable of violence."

"Yes, and Lady Philippa will have no difficulty wrapping a good many influential men around her finger, will she, Mac-Bride?" Sean asked slyly.

Dylan winced inwardly, thinking how Clarinda had had to materialize the police and the fire brigade to free him from the lady's clutches, but he smiled blandly at O'Hara and said merely, "She does have a way about her."

"As I see it," Noel said, "we are going to have to act on our own."

"In what way?" Sean asked.

"Well, first we'll have to get together as many armed and resolute men as we can, then send an expedition to the Circle of Life colony."

"We've got to find it first," Dylan pointed out.

"I know, but your friend Mr. H. has deduced its location as somewhere near the headwaters of the Myrk River, so why not act on that assumption? Unless, of course, you think you can persuade Lady Philippa to divulge the whereabouts of the place."

"I may give it one more try," Dylan said, "but I agree we ought to get going on your idea as soon as possible. Besides armed men, we should gather a store of dynamite and round up as many Gatling guns as possible. What about transport?"

"The *Thunderbolt* has been raised," Noel reported. "Mr. H. and Dr. W. provided large sums of money for the purpose; a competent naval architect, a marine engineer and more shipwrights and welders than I've ever seen in one yard have been hired. They're swarming over that thing like flies right now, practically rebuilding it."

"That's fine," Dylan said, "but what we also need to think about is a way of attacking the Martian landing areas from the air."

"The Naval Air Service isn't interested either," Noel said.

"Perhaps, but you command the *Vengeance* and van Rasselway now has the *Flying Cloud*," Dylan said, "so why not—"

"I think you're about to suggest something that's going to get me court-martialed," Noel said, only half joking.

"Not at all. I was just going to suggest that you might be able to persuade one of your superiors, Commodore Dutton, say, to assign your two ships to manuevers in the Trans-Mortanian area for the next few weeks."

Noel gazed at the tip of his cigar, watching the gray ash while he thought about the suggestion. "Yes, I could put that to Dutton. He's had his eye on Lurleen Shiras, a charming little ballerina I've been meaning to drop from my list. If I were to imply that my absence from the capital would leave the field open to the dashing commodore, he might approve the most improbable kind of maneuvers."

O'Hara laughed. "Depend on my dear brother-in-law to find a way to kill two birds with one stone. Only he could manage to save the Empire and rid himself of an unwanted mistress in one brilliant move."

"How well are the *Vengeance* and *Flying Cloud* armed?" Dylan wanted to know.

"Very lightly," Noel said. "The Board of Admiralty is convinced that airships are for scouting, not for battle. We have a one-pounder and the *Cloud,* which is a little larger, has two."

"I think Churchward could get hold of three or four Gatling guns and a supply of dynamite bombs through his contacts in the industry," Dylan said. "How would your superiors view your taking on some extra armament?"

"As insubordination approaching mutiny," Noel said, finally knocking the ash off his cigar regretfully, "if they knew about it."

"Yes, that's the point, *if* they knew about it," Dylan said. "Suppose six of Churchward's patented rattlers were to be shipped, say, to St. Giles in the Border Marshes, and the same ship carried a supply of those dynamite bombs that were so effective against the Gogs. . . ."

Noel eyed his friend warily. "And?" he prompted.

"And during their maneuvers, the *Vengeance* and *Flying Cloud*, by some strange coincidence, should have to make emergency landings at St. Giles. Then when their minor problems had been attended to, suppose each ship took off armed with three Gatling guns and a cargo of dynamite bombs in addition to their one-pounders. . . . Would anyone be the wiser?"

"Not until after the event," Noel said, "and then the court-martial would convene."

"Even the Admiralty wouldn't be that blind," Dylan said, "when the fate of the human race is at stake."

"You underestimate the myopia of that body," Noel said, "but since it is the very existence of mankind we're talking about—"

"Fine," Dylan said. "Now, how about the men you were talking about? Where do we get our recruits?"

"Volunteers, ex-naval ratings, former rankers from the army," Noel said, "armed by Churchward's merchant-of-death friends and commanded by officers on leave in mufti."

"Good idea," O'Hara said. "There must be thousands of men right here in Avallon who were discharged after the defeat of the Gogs."

"But we don't want just warm bodies with guns," Dylan said. "I'd say former sappers would be most useful since it seems that the most effective way to defeat the Martians is to destroy their capsules before they can open them. Men who can plant charges and dig mines would be our best bet."

"All right. I'll take the responsibility for recruiting them," O'Hara said. "I think St. John and one or two other fellows I know from the Imperial Engineers will help."

"And we'd better get all our plans under way," Dylan

said. "Four more explosions were observed on Thor last night."

Noel drained the last of his whiskey and soda, got to his feet and stretched. "I think I'll pick up van Rasselway at his club and we'll go visit Commodore Dutton's headquarters at Green Fields."

"And I'll go place discreet advertisements in the *Express,* the *Times* and the *Army-Navy Review,*" O'Hara said. "How does this sound: Unattached, fearless former servicemen needed, sappers and miners preferred?"

"Fine," Dylan said with a sigh, "and I suppose I had better rattle Lady Philippa and do my fearless deed also."

Noel raised an eyebrow. "I'm going to beard a despotic commodore in his den and you're off to visit a lovely lady, but you seem to be the one more concerned. I'm not sure I understand that."

"Perhaps because you don't know the lady as well as I do," Dylan said, "and you're not engaged to Clarinda Mac-Tague."

"No, I'm not, you lucky dog," Noel said, "but if you're ever of a mind to pass the lady on, I would—"

"I will never be of that mind," Dylan said a little sharply. "And Clarinda is no little ballerina who would permit herself to be passed from hand to hand."

"No offense, old man, no offense," Noel said jauntily and departed with O'Hara at his heels.

So you're off to see your ladylove again," Clarinda said in his mind when the others were gone.

She's not my ladylove and you know it, Dylan said. *Look what happened last time.*

Clarinda giggled. *Sure now, and she was like to eat you alive, wasn't she?*

No thanks to you, she almost did.

What do you mean, no thanks to me? Didn't I send the police and the firemen to rescue you? What more would you be wantin'? The Imperial Marines maybe?

But why did you wait so long?

Maybe to see how much you'd be tempted, Clarinda said. *It must've been a lot since you're goin' back for a second round.*

I have to go back because my cowardly witch refuses to take a peek into the woman's mind and find out what we need to know.

You didn't call me coward when with nothin' but me mop and bucket I beat off them Gogs that was about to make canapes of you! Nor when I saved you from the great winged beasties on top of that balloon thing! And later when, with the help of Herself, I brought the dynamite into the cave that sent Cythraul to his undeserved rest! Was I coward then?

No, you were the bravest heroine that ever Hibernia produced, Dylan admitted. *As brave and fierce as Scathach the Warrior Witch herself. But that was then and this is now. I'm not asking for all those prodigies of courage, only for a little look into a lady's mind.*

I got a better idea. Why don't you have some of your friends kidnap the wench, take her off in a lonely place—

Clarinda! You ought to be ashamed of yourself!

Twas only a thought, love. I knew you'd rather lallygag with her.

Now, see here— Dylan began indignantly and then realized she was gone as suddenly as she had come.

When he reached Professor Philander's house, he was immediately aware of a change in the atmosphere. The servants were gone and when the professor opened the door himself, he seemed less than pleased to see Dylan.

"You'll find Philippa in the library," he said abruptly, picking up his hat and gloves and preparing to depart.

"Is something wrong, Professor?" Dylan asked, and caught a glint of something in the man's eyes that disturbed him. It wasn't exactly laughter but the kind of grim pleasure a good hater might display on hearing that his worst enemy was going to be drawn and quartered at dawn.

"Something wrong, Mr. MacBride? No, not at all. On the contrary, everything is very right indeed in this best of all possible worlds."

The man left the house, slamming the door rudely behind him, and a puzzled Dylan went into the library to find Lady Philippa kneeling in front of the fireplace tearing up records of some kind and burning them.

"Come in, Dylan," she said coolly. "Come in and sit down. I'd offer you tea or a drink but the servants are all gone."

"Yes, I gathered that when your uncle answered the door," he said, taking a chair near her. "Have you given the help a holiday?"

"No, they have been dismissed," she said quietly. There was no attempt to storm his emotions, no romantic talk about previous lives. It was as though something had happened or was about to happen that made such tactics no longer necessary.

Dylan decided to test his theory. "I've been thinking about some of the things you told me about our mutual past."

"Have you?" she said without a flicker of interest.

"Yes. None of those places where you say we lived and loved are on this planet."

"No," she said, tearing several sheets of paper across and throwing them on the fire. "They're all on Earth."

"Then you're not from Meropis as you said?"

"No." She didn't even look up from her task.

"Then you must have been on Earth, in England, in fact, during the Martian invasion," Dylan said casually, as though just making conversation.

It was a second or two before she seemed to realize what he had said, but then she looked up at him, gray eyes defiant. "Yes, I was. I saw it all."

"It must have been horrifying," Dylan said. "I have read the account by your Mr. Wells and it must have been a greater ordeal than Annwn suffered at the hands of the Gogs."

"It was a terrible time indeed," she said, voice brittle. "A time in which we saw so much promise, such intellectual genius destroyed."

"I don't think I understand," Dylan said.

"Don't you? Then you haven't been listening to what that so-called consulting detective and his doctor friend have been saying about the Circle of Life."

"Yes, I've listened," Dylan said, realizing the cards were all going to be laid on the table now. "I've listened, but I find it hard to believe that there are people who would willingly aid creatures who intend to wipe out the human race."

"And has the human race never wiped out creatures who were less fit to survive?" she demanded. "Even Wells, whose prejudiced, propagandized account of the invasion you and everyone else in Avallon seems to be reading, admits that, doesn't he?"

"I don't know. Does he?"

"Of course he does!" she snapped. "I can quote you the

passage word for word. 'And we men, the creatures who inhabit this earth, must be to them at least as alien and lowly as are the monkeys and lemurs to us. The intellectual side of man already admits that life is an incessant struggle for existence, and it would seem that this, too, is the belief of the minds upon Mars. Their world is far gone into its cooling and this world is still crowded with life, but crowded only with what they regard as inferior animals. To carry war far sunward is, indeed, their only escape from the destruction that, generation after generation, creeps upon them.' "

"I don't think Wells was saying that the Martians had the right to—"

"Listen to what comes next," she said. " 'And before we judge of them too harshly, we must remember what ruthless and utter destruction our own species has wrought, not only upon animals, such as the vanished bison and the dodo, but upon its inferior races. The Tasmanians, in spite of their human likeness, were entirely swept out of existence in a war of extermination waged by European immigrants, in the space of fifty years. Are we such apostles of mercy as to complain if the Martians warred in the same spirit?' "

"Even admitting to man's ruthless nature," Dylan said, "there's no reason to expect the human race to stand meekly waiting for slaughter. And frankly, I wouldn't have thought to find any human being who would ally themselves with the monsters planning that slaughter."

Her lip curled disdainfully. "Who are the monsters, Mr. MacBride, and who the inferior creatures? Who are the worthless bugs that contaminate two worlds upon which vastly superior beings could build a civilization the possibilities of which stagger the mind?"

"Are they superior morally?" Dylan asked.

"Intellectual superiority is synonymous with moral superiority," Philippa said, getting to her feet. "You've only read about it in a book, Dylan. I saw it with my own eyes. The majestic battle machines that swept aside man's feeble resistance, the heat-ray that incinerated hostile gatherings of people as we might burn out a nest of rattlesnakes, the black smoke that sought out and strangled hidden gun crews as we might spray poison to control a plague of wasps. By any Darwinian principles, it was the Martians who deserved to survive, and it was only because of a cruel joke of nature that they were struck down. Most of them died within a few days of each other, you know."

"I understood they all died."

"A few survived a little longer. They crept out of their battle machines, almost helpless, and were set upon by the mobs. I saw them beaten to death with cricket bats, garden hoses and shovels by ignorant Cockneys—stevedores, fishmongers, scullery maids, chimney sweeps—rabble destroying minds so superior to theirs that they were incapable of even conceiving the difference."

"Minds that had massacred hundreds of thousands of those people's fellow citizens," Dylan said.

A gesture of her hand dismissed the deaths caused by the Martians as being of no importance. "We managed to save one of them and keep it alive for a while longer. Yes, even then, we knew which race was the more worthy. Koot Hoomi and Angel Annie brought the desperately ill Martian to the country home of my uncle. There we hid it and fed it the human blood it needed to stay alive."

Dylan stared at her incredulously, eyes wide with horror. "You fed that *thing* human blood?"

She shrugged and looked away. "Yes. It was too bad but we had to sacrifice a chambermaid and a gamekeeper."

"Philippa, I can't believe that you—"

"Why is it any different than killing a brace of rabbits for an honored guest?" she flared. "We did what we had to to keep that great mind alive for as long as we could. The microbes finally killed it, of course, but not before we had all touched its mind and heard it speak to us from the depths of its infinite wisdom."

"You communicated with the Martian?" Dylan asked in spite of his disgust and revulsion at what she was telling him.

"Yes. It was telepathic. When it discovered that some few humans, while not equal to its intelligence, were at least far superior to the cattle around them, it spoke to us. First to Koot Hoomi, then Angel Annie and finally to all of us. It was an experience of unparalleled spirituality, as though we were touching the mind of a god. None of us has ever really been the same since."

"I'm sure," Dylan said, restraining himself with an effort to keep from telling her what he thought of people who would do what she freely admitted. Denouncing the actions and motives of the Circle of Life wasn't going to get him the information he wanted. As long as Philippa seemed inclined to talk, he had better listen. "Communicating with a being from across space must have been fascinating."

Her face lit up and her voice was reverent. "It was like drinking from the fountain of wisdom. Even ill to death as it was, the power of its mind was awe-inspiring. It told us of the preparations to invade Earth, nearly a hundred years of hard work by the whole race. It revealed how the trajectories of the missiles had been plotted, how the great cannon had been built and finally was ready to fire. It fired only a dozen times, however, instead of the hundred that had been intended."

"Why was that?" Dylan asked.

"A defect in the barrel caused the gun to explode and it couldn't be fixed in time for the other missiles to join the invasion force," Philippa said. "Except for that and the unexpected effect of Earth's microbes, the expedition would have been successful. As it was, the most magnificently conceived migration of an entire race was thwarted."

"But now another expedition is on the way?"

"Yes . . . yes, on the way at last!" Her eyes were shining. "Our one survivor told us before it died that it was coming. Six new guns were being constructed and would be ready for firing in a couple of years. Those years have now passed and the Martians are coming again!"

"But the bacteria are still here," Dylan pointed out.

"Ah, but this time they are ready! Before it died, our master taught us how to communicate across space. By the combined power of our minds, we were able to establish telepathic communion with the ruling council on Mars. We offered them our aid and warned of the bacteria menace. We helped them work out defenses against it and arranged to aid them during the initial landings."

"And you've set up a secret colony for that purpose," Dylan said. He was standing face to face with her now, watching the play of emotions across her face, the arrogant pride in what she considered the accomplishments of her group and the worshipful expression every time she spoke of the Martians. He was hoping desperately that those feelings would trick her into betraying the one vital secret. "Where is your base?"

She opened her mouth as though to speak but closed it

again and shook her head. "No, not that. That isn't for you to know. I've told you more than I should have already, even though you'll be able to do nothing with the knowledge." A slight shiver seemed to run through her. "I like you, Dylan. I really do, but we're on opposite sides and I can't let stupid sentiment affect my judgment. If something should go wrong, if you should somehow manage to escape . . ."

She turned away and Dylan stared after her. Had she been threatening him? He took a step toward her, put a hand on her shoulder and turned her around to face him. "What do you mean if I manage to escape? What are you and that gang of yours up to?"

Her smile was sad but resigned. "Dylan, it wasn't my decision to make. If it had been, I might have spared you, but the others were adamant and I came to realize they were right. With the invasion almost on us, you are too dangerous to our plans."

Dylan took a step backward, his hand in his jacket pocket on the cold grip of his revolver. "And how am I to be removed?"

"Koot Hoomi has created a death shadow, an elemental with your name on its lips."

"A what?"

"A cold elemental. A thing of evil and power woven from the fabric of the universe itself. It is mindless and soulless, a creature of negative energy that will engulf you and suck the life essence from you."

"We'll see about that," Dylan said, gripping his revolver tightly as he headed for the door.

"The gun won't do you any good, Dylan," Philippa said. "You can't destroy a negative source of energy with a gun."

Dylan didn't answer, just kept going as fast as his long legs could carry him.

"You can't run from it either, Dylan," she called after him. "It comes to embrace you in its cold deadly arms and you can't escape it."

Chapter 9

Dylan felt the cold as soon as he left the Philander house. He felt the cold and saw the shadow lurking in an alleyway between two buildings as though it was hiding from the last rays of the golden autumn sun. The thing reminded him of a child's clay image of a man, only full-sized and grotesquely misshapen.

With his hand on his revolver, Dylan turned quickly and walked west toward the Silver Strand rather than chance the shortcut through Paradise Gardens toward his apartment. The cold elemental followed, dodging from the shade of a tree to the slender shadow of a lamp post in its efforts to avoid the sun.

It would be dark in about ten minutes, Dylan estimated, and then the thing would attack. If only he could put enough distance between himself and it in the meantime, he might escape.

Rounding the corner onto the broad, tree-lined Arthur's Way, Dylan hurried along trying to keep as much in the light as possible. He was almost running now but neither the people in passing carriages nor the driver of a motor wagon with a load of cotton seemed to notice the long-legged Highland gentleman fleeing before the monstrous slinking shadow.

He thought about calling on Clarinda for help but rejected the idea out of some perverse sense of the proper relationship between the male and female. A man couldn't always be acting like a damsel in distress and relying on his girl to rescue him, could he?

No, he'd fight this one out on his own. After all, the thing hadn't attacked him yet and he did have his thirty-eight in his coat pocket if worst came to worst.

But it was getting dark fast. The sun was a red ball resting on the low-lying hills across the Strand and the buildings were beginning to block its dying rays from the street. As the sun slowly disappeared, the shadowy creature behind Dylan seemed to grow and darken.

Dylan stood for a moment with his back against a light standard and faced the cold elemental. "What is it? What do you want?" he demanded.

There was no answer, but the deeper dark where a face should have been seemed to open and hideous folds that almost resembled lips moved as though forming words. He couldn't hear the words, not even as a whisper, but the movement of the lips made it clear what the thing was saying: *Dylan MacBride.*

That was when Dylan abandoned any thought of dignity and took off at a dead run toward the traffic circle where Arthur's Way joined the esplanade along the Strand. There, without the shadows of trees and buildings, some lingering light might still be left.

The sight of a kilted young man running pell-mell toward the Silver Strand would certainly have attracted the attention of passersby if there had been any, but the usually busy street was all but deserted at this early dining hour. He did pass a motor lorry whose driver shouted something as he went by, and he tried to flag down an empty hack but the cabby refused to stop. No one seemed to see the elemental which was now leaping and bounding from spots of total darkness through lighter patches of shadow in its relentless pursuit.

Dylan could feel the cold more intensely now. It was like a blast of arctic wind against his back. There was also something else, a sound that was so faint it seemed to come from afar, a husky, hollow, whispering sound repeating over and over, "Dylan MacBride, Dylan MacBride."

"Koot Hoomi has created a death shadow," Philippa had said. "A death shadow with your name on its lips."

"We'll see about that!" Dylan muttered, putting on an extra burst of speed. It was brighter here with no trees or buildings and the cold elemental seemed to hang back in the deeper shadows for a few minutes, giving Dylan a chance to put a little more distance between himself and the thing.

But suddenly the sun was gone and dusk settled in over the Strand and the city itself. Looking back over his shoulder, Dylan saw the deadly shade darting after him with remarkable speed, no longer hampered by rays of the setting sun.

"Dylan MacBride . . . Dylan MacBride." The whisper was growing into a sound like the hurrying rush of a freshening wind in a forest glade.

"Got to keep going . . . can't stop now," Dylan panted as he crossed a footbridge over one of the numerous canals that emptied into the Strand. The sound of his boots pounding along the wood decking echoed loudly through the stillness but the hurrying shadow behind him made no sound at all.

It was dark out on the Strand but Dylan could see a low-lying craft of some kind moving north on the tide with its running lights flickering in the mist. At first he thought it might be a large canal barge but then decided it must be a yard oiler when he noticed some kind of superstructure above it.

His breath was coming in painful gasps and he knew he wouldn't be able to run much further. He had to stop if only for a moment or so, but a quick glance over his shoulder told him that even that short a pause would enable the thing, which had grown to three or four times the size of a man, to overtake and envelop him.

"Have to make a stand . . . make a stand with my back to the water," he decided, turning to face the oncoming shadow as he drew his revolver.

"Dylan MacBride, I come, I come." The voice had grown from a whisper to a hoarse shout and the cold the thing radiated was numbing even though it was still perhaps twenty paces away.

"Dylan MacBride, my master says die," the monster was saying as it flowed over the ground toward him.

With a hand shaking from the cold and fear, Dylan lifted his revolver, steadied it against his other arm and fired. There was no way he could have missed his target, but nothing happened. The shot had no effect. The soft-nosed bullet that could shatter human flesh and bone just seemed to disappear in the growing shadow.

"Damn you!" Dylan fired again and again as fast as he could pull the trigger with a finger stiffening from the bitter cold.

"Dylan MacBride, die . . . Master Koot Hoomi says die . . . cold, cold death."

The following slugs had no more effect than the first, and

the elemental was lifting its arms to clasp him in frigid embrace.

"Die . . . die . . . die!" it said as its arms closed about him. He fired the last two rounds in the chamber and then hurled the gun at the thing.

Numbing cold overpowered Dylan. He had spent nights without shelter on the tundra of Basham where even the Gogs sometimes froze in winter, but he had never felt anything like this. The cold gripped him like steel bands, tightening and squeezing until the air was expelled from his lungs and the very blood in his veins seemed to be freezing.

"MacBride? Is that you MacBride?" a voice shouted from somewhere as he tried to struggle in the polar embrace.

"Die . . . die . . . Dylan MacBride! The Circle of Life says die!" the elemental's voice roared in his ear, drowning out the other, more distant voice.

He tried to call out with his mind to Clarinda, to tell her of his love, but the numbing cold was invading his mind and everything was frozen in place.

"I say, what is that thing?" There was a chugging sound like a steam engine but it seemed to come from very faraway, through a frozen mist that would end in death.

"Focus your searchlight on that thing," the precise, slightly accented voice ordered. "Let's see what's going on. You men in the superstructure, stand by the big light!"

The darkness brightened a little and Dylan could see the shadow that enveloped him. It seemed to ripple and even fade a little.

"Keep the light on it!" the voice said again. "Stand by to come about and put a boat over!"

Numbed as he was, Dylan was almost sure that the voice belonged to Mr. H. and the chugging was from a steam engine. He was also sure that the cold elemental was wavering and the pressure of its arms lessening as the light grew brighter. But it was still stronger than he was.

"Die, Dylan MacBride!" the thing said close to his face, its arctic breath searing his lungs.

"Focus both searchlights up there!" the voice ordered. "Keep them trained on that shadowy mass as we come about. Stand by the bow gun, but don't fire unless you can do it without hitting MacBride."

The cold was relaxing its grip on him a little and Dylan found he could move his arms. He tried to shove against the thing that held him and found that it had no substance, just an absence of warmth. The light gave no heat at this distance, but it still seemed to weaken the cold elemental.

The cold steel bands that were its arms slipped from around Dylan and he was able to throw himself backward into the water. Plunging into the water that would ordinarily have seemed chill was like diving into a warm bath after the frigid grip of the death shadow. For a few moments Dylan let himself sink into it, allowing the relative warmth to start his blood circulating and bring back strength to his arms. Then he somehow managed to struggle out of his coat and surface in time to see the cold elemental slowly fading into nothingness under the combined glare of the ship's two powerful searchlights.

"MacBride, are you all right?" It was Dr. W. in the bow of the *Thunderbolt's* longboat shoving a boat hook out for Dylan to grasp.

"Y-yes, j-just g-get m-me on b-board and p-pour some br-brandy d-down me," Dylan said between chattering teeth. "L-let me s-sit in the boiler r-room for a couple of h-hours and I'll b-be f-fine."

"Well, old boy, that was a near thing," Dr. W. said as he and two seamen hauled Dylan up into the boat. "What was that dreadful shadowy thing?"

"A d-death shadow," Dylan said. "A c-cold elemental c-conjured up by K-Koot Hoomi."

Then the longboat was bumping against the turtlelike side of the *Thunderbolt* and the seamen were helping him up a rope ladder.

"It is to welcome you aboard the new super-extra *Thunderbolt*, Mr. MacBride," Professor Lombosa said, giving him a hand as he reached the top.

"G-glad to be aboard, Professor," Dylan said, shivering as he looked around at the changes in the diving ram. A six-pounder, rapid-fire gun had been mounted aft and a four-inch rifle forward. There were two Gatling guns, one on a deckhouse that had been built behind the conning tower and the other set up behind the forward gun. The ship's freeboard had been raised also so that instead of shoving her bow sluggishly into any slight waves, she rode over them.

"It is almost stable now," Mr. H. said, looming up behind Lombosa, "and the engines might even move her against the tide."

"You've done wonders," Dylan said.

"We had wondrous amounts of money to do it with, H. said. "My older brother saw to it that the royal exchequer was open to us without stint."

"You mean you went back through the Shimmering Gates to Earth for funds?" Dylan asked, accepting a stiff brandy from Dr. W. and letting the fiery stuff melt the ice particles he was sure were floating in his veins.

"No, we had a contingency fund with us in the form of bank drafts against Lloyds of Avallon. It is interesting that the august institution of Lloyds has branches on both sides of the Shimmering Gates."

"It seems that on your world, as well as ours, large financial interests have a way of getting what they want," Dylan said, finishing his brandy and pulling the blanket someone had draped over his shoulder close around him.

"By the way, MacBride, have you learned anything from Lady Philippa?" H. asked.

Dylan shook his head, half expecting icicles to drop off the tips of his ears. "Nothing about the hidden base, but something about their relationship with the Martians."

"That's too bad," H. said. "She was our last chance. The others are all gone from the city. While I was busy with the *Thunderbolt*, the others eluded the men I hired to watch them. I fear they have all fled to the secret base. Has she gone too, do you know?"

"She was burning papers and records while I talked to her," Dylan said. "She only told me as much as she did because she was sure the death shadow Koot Hoomi created would kill me before I could talk to anyone."

"Just what did you learn?" Dr. W. asked, taking Dylan's pulse.

Dylan told them of Lady Philippa's near worship of the Martians, of the way the Circle of Life had hidden one of the creatures and learned to communicate across the vast distances of space with the invaders.

"Yes, I surmised they were able to do something like that," H. said. "Our savants had theories that mental telepathy was the natural means of communication between the Martians themselves."

"But I'm afraid we're on our own about the colony," Dylan said. "She wouldn't say a word about that. I guess we'll just have to go search for it."

"With only H.'s deductive reasoning to guide us," Dr. W. said.

"Unless Miss Clarinda could be persuaded to . . ." H. suggested.

"No, I can't imagine anything that would persuade her to touch their minds," Dylan said regretfully. "I've tried everything I can think of."

"But you will prevail upon the lady to accompany us on the *Thunderbolt* into the interior of Avallon, won't you?"

"I'll do my best," Dylan promised. "Is the *Thunderbolt* ready to sail?"

"We have already taken on provisions and ammunition," Lombosa said proudly. "It is the fuel docks we now approach."

"We ship our fighting crew in the morning, MacBride," H. said. "Can you and your lady be aboard by noon?"

"Yes," Dylan said. "I'll have Clarinda on board if I have to tell her we're just going on a picnic to one of the islands of Lake Regillos."

Dr. W. chuckled. "Some picnic, in the wilds of Tir-Narog on the banks of the Myrk River."

"Where, if my powers of deductive reasoning have not failed me, we will find the Circle of Life and their hidden base," H. said.

Chapter 10

The *Thunderbolt* was alongside the coal docks in the Silver Strand, her bunkers being filled by her crew and dock workers, when Dylan and Clarinda arrived in a hired brougham. The priestess was dressed in a smart gray traveling suit and feathered hat but unlike most young ladies setting out on a trip of undetermined length, she was not overburdened with luggage. All she had brought along was two changes of clothing and a basic supply of her magical paraphernalia, but she was loaded down with doubts and complaints.

"How do you know the sinkin' boat won't sink again?" she demanded, eyeing the craft suspiciously as Dylan helped her out of the brougham.

"It's been completely rebuilt under the supervision of a competent naval architect, and Professor Lombosa is turning over the actual command to me."

"Sure now, and what would you be knowin' of sinkin' boats?"

"I'm a qualified ship's master," Dylan said, "and I've commanded expeditions in seas that would make those on the inland waters look like rain puddles."

She gave him a roguish glance over her shoulder as they started up the gangplank. "Then we won't be needin' to hire a captain for our yacht when you take me on a honeymoon cruise to the far Green Seas, will we?"

"I'm afraid that will have to wait until after we send the Martians packing."

"Or after they've packed us in syrup for sale in whatever passes for butcher shops on Thor," she said.

Dylan stopped and turned her to face him. "Have you seen something, Clarinda? Has Keridwen told you something in the cauldron?"

She shook her head. "No, 'cause I've not looked into it. I'm not so fond of gazin' into me own future since I seen us dyin' in Cythraul's cavern."

"But we didn't die," Dylan pointed out.

"No, but you had to go gallivantin' off to that awful place with me trailin' after you like a lovesick calf," she said. "Just what was the likes of Clarinda MacTague doin' facin' up to old ugly-face Cythraul?"

"Who better? Aren't you the Annwnian avatar of Keridwen, All Mother?"

"I never claimed any such thing!" she said indignantly. "I never claimed to deal in anything more important than an occasional love charm or maybe a tiny geas on somebody's stepmother to help a romance along."

"But you have done things that only a goddess could do," Dylan said. "Like transporting the dynamite that destroyed Cythraul's caves and propelling yourself through space and time."

"Are you seriously thinkin' that I'm a goddess, love?"

"Only in appearance, love," Dylan teased. "What I'm saying is that you seem to have the franchise on the great lady's miracles for this planet."

"Miracles, is it?" She grinned. "How can you be knowin' it's not just the result of clean livin' and moral fortitude?"

"Welcome aboard, skipper," the young first officer greeted Dylan with a snappy salute.

"Good to be aboard, Mr. Asbury," Dylan said, returning the salute and smiling at the young man's admiring glance in Clarinda's direction. "This is Miss MacTague, my fiancée."

"A pleasure, ma'am," Asbury murmured, bending over to kiss the hand the redhead extended.

"Is the full crew on board, Mr. Asbury?" Dylan asked.

"Yes, sir, except for a working party that accompanied the second officer and the bos'n in the longboat to bring away the, ahem, recruits."

"Passengers," Dylan corrected. "Let's call them passengers while we're still alongside." He wondered what the government's attitude would be to an unauthorized armed ship carrying off equally well-armed ex-servicemen.

"Yes, sir," Asbury said and stood aside while Dylan escorted Clarinda below to one of the four tiny cabins that had been constructed beneath the conning tower and deckhouse.

She looked around at the cubbyhole, hands on hips, shaking her head. "Are you thinkin' I can be folded up to fit in this mouse hole? Is it this I gave up me warm, snug bed in Trogtown for? I'm a big girl and I wasn't raised to sleep on a shelf like you Sassenach seagoers."

"That's a perfectly adequate bunk and at least you'll have privacy," Dylan said. "The other passengers and crew members will be jammed into a forecastle the size of an ordinary ship's galley."

"And where will yourself be sleepin'?" she asked, stepping cautiously into the small cabin. "Would we be after havin' adjoinin' rooms maybe?"

"As captain, my cabin will be in the deckhouse behind the conning tower."

"Ah, it will? What a way to spend a honeymoon," she said.

"This isn't exactly a honeymoon," Dylan said. "There's that little matter of a marriage ceremony yet."

"You mean one of your cold Sassenach ceremonies?

You'll be rememberin' that we are sealed in Keridwen's love already."

"Yes, there was that, wasn't there?" Dylan said, turning toward the ladder to go back topside.

"Being captain of this vessel, such as it is, you'd be empowered to marry a couple all proper and lawlike, wouldn't you?" she called after him.

Dylan paused halfway up the ladder and looked back at her. "I suppose I would be, but you're forgetting that even a captain can't preside at his own wedding."

"Ah, I knew he'd be findin' a way to squirm out of it," Clarinda said, lifting her eyes heavenward. "You heard that, didn't you, Keridwen? Heard this fellow you wished on me refuse your own priestess, me who has always worshiped you nice and proper!"

Dylan grinned at her histrionics. "I'll talk to you later. I have to see about preparations for getting under way."

"The longboat is approaching, sir, with our . . . passengers," Asbury told him as he stuck his head up through the hatch. "Major Churchward and his two friends are already on board and Professor Lombosa is in the engine room with the new chief engineer."

Dylan nodded and went up the ladder into the conning tower and out onto the little makeshift flying bridge from which the ship could be conned when she wasn't in action.

Mr. H. was already there studying a map.

"Do we have a course?" Dylan asked.

The tall, keen-eyed man nodded. "A course plotted out by deductive reasoning and evidence to lead us to our enemies' lair," H. said, unfolding the map and displaying it on the small chart table. "We proceed to the south on the Silver Strand from Avallon and into Lake Regillos. We coal at Caer Kari on Lake Camlam and proceed through the Midlands Canal into the Medelgo River. We coal again at Pilgrim's Rest and then proceed upriver to St. Rory where the tributary Myrk River joins the Medelgo. Then up the Myrk to its headwaters where, without doubt, we will find the Circle of Life's base."

"Without a doubt," Dylan said, his mind filled with doubts.

The quartermaster came up the ladder and handed a folded message to Dylan. "Telegram from Captain Bran ap Lynn."

Dylan opened the paper and read: *Negotiations for de-*

ployment of Vengeance *and* Flying Cloud *successful. A certain young lady has a new protector and two airships a new mission. When in all respects ready for sea proceed to rendezvous at St. Rory.*

"What's that about a young lady?" Clarinda demanded, having approached without a sound to stand peering over his shoulder.

"Ah, just that one of Noel's lights of love has been retired, so to speak," Dylan said.

"For sure he'll be gettin' his comeuppance from some little beauty who'll put a lock and key on him some day," Clarinda predicted.

"I thought you were unpacking and putting your things away," Dylan said.

"Indeed? I've only three shifts to me name, but even supposin' I had more, where do you think I'd be puttin' them in that crevice you've assigned me?"

"Second officer and boat crew aboard now, sir," Asbury reported.

"Hoist in the longboat," Dylan ordered. "Set special sea detail and stand by to get under way."

Dylan was in his element now. The command of a ship, even such a clumsy, clunking craft as this diving ram, had always thrilled him. As soon as the longboat was aboard and secured, he stepped to the wing of the bridge where he could see the men at the lines.

"Haul up on your spring line," he ordered and followed with, "let go aft," and finally, "let go forward."

As the *Thunderbolt* moved away from the dock, Dylan stepped to the speaking tube and passed the word to the engine room and conning tower. "All back one-third. Helmsman, sound one long blast on the air horn."

The *Thunderbolt* was on its way at last, backing out into the main stream of the estuary; with a word of command from Dylan and the clanging of the engine room telegraph, it stopped and then lurched forward at a brisk five knots.

"I think I'm going to be seasick," Clarinda said when the craft began to hit a slight swell in the estuary.

"Perhaps some spirits of ammonia," Dr. W. suggested, hurrying to her side.

"A little spirits of gin would be more soothing," the priestess said, "with just a wee bit of tonic."

The hundred miles across Lake Regillos and the almost

three hundred miles up the length of Lake Camlam were un-
eventful. After coaling at Caer Kari, the ram passed through
the thirty miles of the Midlands Canal. Once into the great
Medelgo River, which was several miles wide at some spots,
the *Thunderbolt* began to have problems. Even the new engines weren't up to making headway against the strong current and it soon became apparent the ship could only manage to maintain her position. The longboat was launched
and Asbury and Churchward went ashore to a big, sprawling
river town and obtained the services of a tug which soon
came alongside and threw lines to the ram. With the tug's
powerful engines added to her own, the *Thunderbolt* proceeded upstream to the border barony of St. Rory. There,
in the port of the same name, she again took on coal.

The *Vengeance* and *Flying Cloud* arrived the next day,
and Noel and van Rasselway came aboard to hold one last
council of war.

"There were five more explosions on Thor the day we left
Avallon," Noel reported, "and the Senate adjourned for the
holiday and the Emperor left for Pleasure Island in Lake
Tethys."

"In other words, the Martians are coming in force and the
government is responding with a vigorous yawn," Dylan said.

It was decided that the *Thunderbolt* would proceed up the
mysterious Myrk River to search along its banks for an area
that corresponded to the physical evidence Mr. H. had found
in Koot Hoomi's rooms. The two airships would remain near
St. Rory until the Circle of Life base was found and they
were summoned via telegraph for the attack on the enemy.

"Let us hope we're in time," Dr. W. said. "If we arrive
to find the Martians landed, out of their capsules and into
their battle machines, all will have been in vain."

"It's too bad we don't have a faster way of finding the
base," Dylan said with a significant look at Clarinda.

The redhead shook her head stubbornly. "No! You
wouldn't ask if you knew what it was like. It would freeze
me soul to touch their minds."

"Then we must depend on deduction," Mr. H. said with
hardly a trace of regret in his precise voice.

The *Thunderbolt* headed her ram bow into the Myrk
River early the next morning and headed west. At first the
water, shallow and flowing sluggishly, was about the same
color as that of the Medelgo, but on the second day it be-

gan to change and grow darker. Heavy deposits of minerals gave it a gray look that shaded off almost into black because of the tall trees growing on both banks and shutting out the sun except at midday.

"Aye, shivery place, it is," Clarinda said, staring up at the gigantic hundred-foot-high trees and the curtains of moss that hung from them. "A place you might expect them Martian octopussies to hide out in, along with trolls and dragons."

"I don't recall ever seeing any trolls in these parts, ma'am," the guide Dylan had hired at St. Rory spoke up. He was a stoop-shouldered, balding little man with bristling black whiskers and arms that almost seemed to touch the ground as he walked. Aptly named Long-Arm Gibbon, he wore a buckskin shirt and a double bandolier across his chest. He was never seen without his single-shot rifle or the knife he kept on his belt. "Never seen no dragons neither, but there's lots of Skerlings and an occasional blue-painted Pict and either one of 'em would as soon take your scalp or split your skull open to suck out your brains as they would look at you."

Clarinda looked accusingly at Dylan. "The things a woman gets herself into when she falls in love! There I was with me nice little business in charms and spells and me happy little brood of brothers and sisters and what did I have to do? I had to fall in love with a kilted Sassenach barbarian and go traipsin' all over lookin' to get me scalp lifted by bloodthirsty, befeathered savages!"

"I hear tell the Skerlings are partial to red hair," Gibbon said, spitting tobacco juice overboard after testing the wind with a raised wet finger, " 'specially long red hair."

"Oh, Dylan, will you still love me when I'm bald as Mr. Gibbon?"

"Of course, sometimes they just carry off the women," Gibbon said. "Carry 'em off and torture 'em just for the pleasure of hearin' 'em scream."

Dylan wished the man would shut up. Clarinda was nervous enough without being terrorized further. But as he saw the glitter in the girl's eyes, he realized she wasn't being taken in completely.

"Yes, sir, some of the things I've heard that them fellas did to a woman, you wouldn't want to happen to your mother-in-law," Long-Arm said, testing the wind and getting ready to spit again.

Dylan knew what was going to happen when Clarinda's eyes took on a sudden intense look. Long-Arm spat with the wind behind him, tobacco and juice propelled from his mouth in a dark brown stream. The wind freshened, abruptly changed direction and blew the tobacco back into his face, splattering it from bald head to whiskers.

While Long-Arm wiped at the mess with a checkered handkerchief, Clarinda smiled sweetly. "I hear tell there are wind elementals in these parts that can change a north wind to a south wind without even puffin' up their cheeks."

"Can't understand it . . . sure can't understand it," Long-Arm said and crossed to the port side of the ship.

The Myrk River grew even darker as it came into the shadow of the awesome Mountains of Forever and paralleled them on a northward curve until it plunged through Hell's Gate, a deep, sheer-walled canyon the river had carved through the mountains themselves. Beyond Hell's Gate, the river narrowed to such an extent that the branches of the giant trees on either side entwined to form a canopy through which only a dim light filtered.

The *Thunderbolt* and the tug had to use their searchlights to navigate and the danger of running aground became such that Dylan seldom left the bridge.

"One can imagine almost any kind of menace lurking in such a dark, treacherous tunnel," Dr. W. remarked one afternoon as the pointed ram at the *Thunderbolt*'s bow cleaved through the murky water and the wind whispered spookily through the living ceiling.

What was lurking along the banks of the Myrk River was Picts, blockading the river with two huge cut trees. They appeared without warning on both banks, hundreds of blond-haired and bearded men, nearly naked bodies tattooed blue, and began bombarding the *Thunderbolt* with a hail of arrows and rocks. The helmsman was hit and collapsed in front of the wheel. The lookout forward and the man taking soundings beside him were both struck by arrows and went overboard.

The ram started to swing broadside to the current and the tug following behind fouled her. Mr. Asbury took the helm himself and Dylan yelled for the crew to man their battle stations. But there was more to contend with than arrows and rocks. A score or more round wickerwork boats filled with screeching Picts armed with battle-axes and swords pushed out from the reeds along the bank.

"Get the Gatling guns going!" Churchward shouted, coming on deck in his long johns, pulling on his pants with one hand and trying to fire a revolver with the other. Before the crew of the ram could get topside, the seemingly clumsy but actually handy wickerwork boats were slamming against the ship's iron sides and the Picts were coming aboard hand over hand, axes slung over their backs and short, swordlike daggers gripped in their teeth.

Dylan was on the wing of the bridge with revolver in hand and Clarinda crouched beside him. He saw a Pict reach the main deck and grapple with a seaman armed only with a belaying pin. Other seamen were popping out of the deckhouse and hatches armed with cutlasses and pistols but the Picts were overwhelming in their numbers and fighting as ferociously as Gogs.

"Get your men on deck, Lieutenant Reardon!" Dylan yelled to the officer in command of the twenty-five ex-servicemen they had shipped as marines. "Get your men on deck with bayonets fixed."

A Pict cut down the seaman who was trying to defend the deckhouse, then began stabbing at Asbury through the portholes of the conning tower with a spear. Dylan shot him between the eyes and grabbed up a cutlass a seaman had dropped as a dozen other blue-painted barbarians swarmed up on the deckhouse and made for the hatch of the conning tower and flying bridge where he and Clarinda crouched.

"Oh, Keridwen, sweet mither of mine, look what you've got me into this time!" the witch girl moaned. "You and your love stuff are goin' to get your only workin' priestess scalped or her head chopped open, whichever it is these naked savages is partial to!"

Ten fingers tattooed blue got a grip on the wooden railing surrounding the flying bridge and the Pict they belonged to started to hoist himself up onto it. Praying under her breath, Clarinda cracked his knuckles with the heel of her shoe until he yelled in pain and crashed back onto the deck.

Dylan shot three more as they rushed the conning tower and bridge. He put a bullet through the hand of another who was trying to pry open the hastily closed, undogged hatch of the conning tower with a sword blade. Turning, Dylan saw an arm go back to throw a spear in his direction.

He aimed the gun hastily and pulled the trigger only to hear it click on an empty chamber. For a moment he found himself staring at what seemed certain death as the spear left the Pict's hand and hurtled toward him. Then the weapon slowed and hovered in midair, turning in a lazy circle and burying itself in the arm of the man who had thrown it.

"Ha! Them wind elementals are at it again," Clarinda said.

Other hands and heads were appearing over the edge of the flying bridge. Dylan didn't have time to reload his revolver so he attacked with the cutlass, tumbling one barbarian overboard with a split skull and slicing another's shoulder open.

As that one's ax clattered on the deck, Clarinda whimpered and went for it on her hands and knees. A hairy-legged Pict leaped over the rail and landed on it first. The redhead got both hands on the handle of the ax and lifted, sending the Pict staggering back against the rail.

In close combat with two other savages, Dylan could spare Clarinda only a quick glance. He saw her snatch up the ax as the Pict came toward her with lifted dagger. Using the weapon like a battering ram, she jammed the head of it into the man's middle and sent him head over heels into the river. Recovering quickly, she turned on another attacker who came leaping over the opposite rail, catching him beside the head with the blunt edge of the ax and felling him in his tracks.

Dylan cut down one of his opponents and Churchward shot another. Mr. H. and Dr. W. had managed to get inside the conning tower and were firing out through the portholes with good effect, but most of the crew was either dead or trapped below by groups of Picts who commanded the hatchways.

Churchward tried to make his way forward to the bow Gatling gun but was blocked by several of the savages. He fell back, firing until his revolver was empty, then threw it into the face of a big, blue-painted chieftain who hurled a war ax at him but missed. Mr. H. shot two of Churchward's attackers, and Dr. W. opened the hatchway a crack, tossed the major a loaded gun and slammed it shut in the faces of half a dozen Picts who immediately began chopping at the iron with their razor-sharp blades.

With Clarinda beside him, Dylan had managed to clear the bridge, but the rest of the ship was aswarm with wild blond men who kept pouring onto the deck from the wicker boats alongside.

Clarinda was screeching at the Picts like the Warrior Witch herself. "Come on, you bloody-minded, purple-skinned fiends! Come on and see what you'll have to pay for a strand of MacTague hair!" She swung the heavy ax around her head as though it were light as a feather, red hair flying like a battle flag. "Come on and see how you like the feel of me ax! And see how you like the geas and the hexes I'm gonna lay on you and you get for a thousand generations just as soon as I remember the proper words."

Some Picts were gathered in the bow and amidship getting orders from their war leaders. Others were crawling aft to where Churchward had taken shelter behind the shield of the Gatling gun and was trying to open the ready ammo box. Someone had put a padlock on the box and the major was trying to shoot it off while the savages swarmed toward him and Mr. H. and Dr. W. fired at their broad backs.

Dylan leaped to the speaking tube and whistled up Lombosa in the engine room. "All full ahead!" he shouted. "Give me everything you've got, Professor! I'm going to ram my way through that barrier in the river!"

The tug, which had had enough speed to elude most of the boarding boats, and whose crew had driven off the few Picts who had gained their deck, came chugging up behind the *Thunderbolt* to help.

Dylan picked up the megaphone and shouted to the tug's skipper, "Stand by to give us a push! I'm going to ram the blockade!"

Churchward had the ammo tub open and was jamming a magazine into the Gatling gun but keeping a wary eye on his would-be attackers.

The Gatling gun would be devastating against the Picts in the boats alongside or those in the boats still hurrying toward the ram from either bank, but it would be useless against those already swarming on deck. Only the crew and marines trapped below could clear the savages from the decks, but even they couldn't do much if all the Picts heading for the *Thunderbolt* managed to get aboard. That was why Dylan knew he had to get the ram under way and leave them behind, clear targets for the machine gun.

"They're comin' after us again, love!" Clarinda shouted as a score of blond devils came charging from the bow, hurling spears and axes as they came. Dylan pulled the redhead down beside him and again emptied his revolver into the mass of screeching fiends. Several went down and the others hesitated as the *Thunderbolt* lurched forward, heading for the barrier in the river.

Clarinda was on her hands and knees, eyes tightly shut and lips moving. In a brief lull in the screaming and gunfire, Dylan heard part of her words:

"By Keridwen's snow-white bosom and Avvadug's freezin' breath, by the circlin' of the moons and the risin' of the sun, send me a curse, oh spirits of wind and air! Send me a curse such as the Picts will be rememberin' as long as they tell each other lies over the cook fires in their mud and wattle huts! Send me a plague out of Uffern that will make their teeth fall out and the blood run backward in their veins; send little beasties that will bite them with teeth like daggers!"

A thrown ax just missed Dylan and a spear plunked into the deck beside Clarinda's leg. She screamed and opened her eyes as the Picts swarmed up onto the bridge in overwhelming numbers.

"Send it, blast you, send it or get yourself a new priestess —if you can find one stupid enough to worship a careless goddess who lets her only dependable girl get into these scrapes!" Clarinda yelled, hacking away at the Picts with her ax while Dylan slashed with his cutlass.

Then several things happened at once. A sword knocked Clarinda's ax out of her hand, Dylan's cutlass refused to pull free from the belly of its latest target and the *Thunderbolt*'s ram struck the first of the two tree trunks with such force that the resulting shock wave knocked everyone down.

Tree branches came crashing onto the deck, but with the engines of both the ram and the tug straining to the utmost, they pushed the huge tree aside and plowed into the second one.

The Picts were all over Dylan and Clarinda and he was struggling to keep one of them from stabbing the girl. She had grabbed one long blond braid, dragged its owner down on deck and was trying to strangle him with his own hair while she kicked frantically at another wild-eyed warrior who had gotten hold of her leg and was trying to plunge his sword into her back.

"Keridwen, do it! Do it quick, me lady! I know you

don't like violence but we need some right now if you're goin' to have a priestess left to your name!"

Dylan tumbled the man with the sword backward off the bridge and Clarinda let go the one she was strangling to sink her teeth into the wrist of a Pict trying to knife Dylan between the shoulder blades.

"Do it, you old biddie, or I'll join up with Avvadug's devil worshipers!" the priestess howled, and suddenly there was a sound like the buzzing of a million bees.

A blue-painted savage trying to decapitate Dylan suddenly dropped his ax and bellowed in pain, hitting frantically at something that seemed to have buried itself in his rump. Another Pict began to swat at a large golden insect that had become attached to the end of his nose. Others all around them suddenly lost all interest in murdering Clarinda and her lover as they howled and slapped at the golden bugs.

"She's doin' it!" Clarinda said gleefully. "There you go, me buckos! I warned you but you wouldn't listen, so now feel them kisses from me and Keridwen!"

The *Thunderbolt* lurched again and her ram slipped under the second tree and pushed it aside as the Picts began to jump overboard. The sharp clatter of the Gatling gun added its share to the din of screams, pistol shots and the snapping of branches.

Dylan was reaching for Clarinda to kiss her when he felt something like the point of a red hot needle sink into his shoulder. The pain was excruciating and he suddenly knew why the Picts were swarming overboard as the golden insects buzzed around them.

"Not him, you idiot, not him!" Clarinda shouted. "Keridwen, you lovesick mooncalf, sting them, not us!"

The stinging pain ceased as quickly as it had begun and Dylan started forward, one arm around Clarinda and the other gripping his pistol, to check the damage to his ship. The last of the Picts leaped into the water and the Gatling gun sent the wicker boats scurrying.

A hatch opened almost at Dylan's feet and a bald head came into view followed by Long-Arm Gibbon's enormous buffalo rifle. "Where are they? Where's them heathens gone to? If I hadn't been dogged in down below, they'd never of dared! Run off, have they? Heard I was here, eh? They never would have attacked in the first place if they'd knowed the best Skerling scout of them all was on board!"

Clarinda rolled her eyes heavenward. "Keridwen, me love, if you should happen to have one more sting left, would you be puttin' it where I wish it would go?"

Gibbon let out a howl that drowned out the yells of the retreating Picts and slapped wildly at his bald head, lost his footing and went tumbling down the ladder onto the lower deck.

"Oh, what a pity!" Clarinda said, nuzzling Dylan's ear. "One of them things of Keridwen's must have thought he was a bald-headed Pict, what with them whiskers and all."

Chapter 11

The *Thunderbolt* headed upstream through an increasingly narrow and shoaling river. Dylan, Churchward, Dr. W. and Mr. H. were on the flying bridge with binoculars trained on the shore during most of the daylight hours. At night searchlights were kept trained on either bank. The chartered tug churned along close astern, ready to render assistance any time the ram's cranky engines acted up.

The close watch maintained on the thickly forested banks was for two purposes: one was to give warning of another attack by Picts or Skerlings, the other to locate the precise geological and floral combination Mr. H. predicted for the site of the hidden colony.

In addition to the search along the river, Long-Arm Gibbon hired four friendly Skerlings as scouts and took them with him to search the hinterland for tracks or any other sign of the Circle of Life members.

After almost a week of such activity, everyone on board the *Thunderbolt* was beginning to sense that they weren't going to find the colony along the Myrk River. Everyone but Mr. H., that is. He still wasn't ready to give up.

"It is eminently reasonable that the colony is somewhere along this river," he told Dylan and Churchward the morning the man with the lead line reported there was no longer enough water to float even the shallow-draft ram. "Geological formations and flora of the type of which I found traces in Koot Hoomi's rooms occur only along such waterways, and we did trace Lady Philippa's movements as far as St. Rory. We also know that she chartered a steam launch there and headed into the Medelgo."

"But we don't know if she turned into the Myrk or proceeded on upstream toward the headwaters of the Medelgo," Churchward pointed out.

"No, that isn't possible," H. said. "MacBride, didn't you tell me that the headwaters of the Medelgo lay somewhere in the Great North Plains?"

Dylan nodded. "Grasslands, almost like tundra in some areas. Totally unlike this area."

"Then we'll wait for the return of Gibbon and his Skerling scouts," H. said. "He's bound to have found something by now."

"In my opinion, Long-Arm Gibbon would have trouble finding an elephant at a circus, much less a secret base," Dylan said.

"He'll find something," H. said confidently. "I can't be wrong; I just can't be."

But Long-Arm Gibbon's return produced only disappointment. He not only hadn't found anything, he had led his men into a hive of bees.

"Him big blundering idiot," the Skerling chief told Dylan through lips swollen by bee stings. "Skerlings hunt in land for hundreds of moons and never get stung by bees. Long-Arm get all stung in one day."

"Gentlemen, we are faced with defeat," H. told them after lengthy consultations with Gibbon and the Skerling chief. "Not only defeat, but disaster. My deductive reasoning has led us astray."

"But surely not, old boy," Dr. W. protested. "Perhaps we have missed something along the way. Let us retrace our steps and—"

"No, it is hopeless. The colony is not on the Myrk River, although I am sure the base would have to be on a navigable river in order to bring in construction materials and supplies."

"They wouldn't have to be on no river if they had a flying machine," Gibbon said between mouthfuls of beans and sour belly.

"A flying machine? You mean an airship?" Dylan asked.

"Don't rightly sound like no airship," the scout said, "not the way the Skerlings described it."

"What are you talking about?" H. demanded, striding over to Gibbon and gripping his arm. "What the devil do you mean? What did the Skerlings describe?"

"That flying machine they been seeing the last few months. They told me about it when they first came along."

"Why didn't you tell us this before?" Dylan asked angrily.

Gibbon looked affronted. "You didn't say you was looking for no flying machine."

"What did it look like?" H. asked. "Describe it for us, please."

Gibbon pulled his arm away. "Get the chief's son to show you that picture he drawed on buffalo hide, if you're interested." He went back to chewing noisily on a piece of hardtack.

The Skerlings, who had absolutely refused to go on board the *Thunderbolt*, were squeezed together near the bow of the tug eating. Dylan and his friends jumped from the stern of the ram onto the tug's deck and hurried to them.

"Lean Buck," Dylan said to the chief's son. "Do you have a drawing of a machine that flies in the sky?"

The young Skerling looked at his father and when the older man nodded took a piece of cured buffalo hide out of a pouch at his belt and handed it over. Dylan stared at the round winged object drawn on it and handed the hide to Mr. H.

"I've never seen anything that looked like that," he said.

"I have," H. said. "There's one in the British Museum, in fact."

"Yes, it's a Martian flying machine," Dr. W. said.

"And very well depicted," H. said, handing the drawing back to the young Skerling. "Where did you see this thing?"

"Over there, many leagues and a few leagues," Lean Buck said, sweeping his arm toward the west in a semicircle.

"Over there," his father said, pointing north, "many times."

"That way." Another Skerling pointed east.

"And that way," the fourth man said, pointing south.

"That's just fine," Dylan muttered. "All points of the compass."

"If it's been flitting around everywhere," Churchward said thoughtfully, "perhaps it was searching for a landing site for itself or—"

"For the Martians!" Dylan finished for him.

H. seemed depressed and melancholy as they returned to the *Thunderbolt*. "I have misled all of us, gentlemen," he said. "I should have realized the difference between this world and my own. This is a place of myth, legend and magic, not reason and logic. On Earth magic is nothing but the imaginings of immature minds, but here it works. The powers of logic and deductive reasoning that I have so fully developed do not serve me well on Annwn. Consequently, I have misled us and we have wasted valuable time in this futile search."

"But we have gained new information," Dylan said. "We now know that the Circle of Life uses a Martian flying machine to reach their base and probably to keep it supplied. Perhaps we could have one of our airships follow it to its lair and—"

"Hopeless," H. said. "Theirs is capable of speeds of hundreds of miles an hour through some means of propulsion that Earth's scientists have not as yet been able to understand. It would simply flit away from airships, unless, of course, they could spot it on the ground."

"There's something else we haven't considered," Churchward said in a worried voice. "Does the presence of this flying machine mean that some Martians have already landed?"

Everyone looked at Mr. H., who thought for a few minutes with his pointed chin in his hand before shaking his head. "If anyone still trusts my deductive power, I would say no."

"Of course we trust you," Dylan said. "Being wrong once in a lifetime doesn't make you an imbecile. I'd wager most of us are wrong at least once a day."

H. shook his head gravely. "I'm afraid this has shattered my confidence badly. But for what it's worth, I think the Circle of Life found the craft on Earth and were able to learn to operate it through their telepathic communications with the Martians. They must have brought it through the Shimmering Gates with them."

"That must have cost a pretty penny in life-force," Churchward said, remembering his own trip through the Gates and

how heavily the priestess who had come with him had paid
for the privilege of bringing a Gatling gun from Earth.

"Yes, unless they know of another way," H. said. "Another set of Gates."

"There have been rumors to that effect," Dylan said. "But
this isn't solving our problem. What are we going to do?"

"As I see it," Churchward said, "we're never going to find
the secret base unless Miss Clarinda is willing to help."

They all looked at Dylan and he sighed. "I'll go talk to her
again."

"Talk to her about what?" Clarinda asked from the open
hatchway of the deckhouse. "If it's lookin' into them mechanical minds, it won't do any good. For anyone with
the power, and especially a priestess of Keridwen, to go
muckin' around in minds without any emotion at all could
be disastrous. It's like hot lead hittin' cold water."

Dylan could partially understand her reluctance and he
didn't want any harm to come to her, but with the fate of
two worlds and all of mankind hanging in the balance,
someone had to do something.

"Very well," Dylan said, "you know what you can and
can't do. Why don't I try something else. Lady Philippa has
some small ability to pick up other people's thoughts, so
why don't I try to project mine and—"

"You'll do nothin' of the kind, Dylan MacBride," Clarinda
said, hands on hips and violet eyes flashing fire. "You
keep out of that woman's mind or I'll put a geas on you
that'll make your kilts fall off every time you pass a lady
on the street! I'll get your information but not by touchin'
minds. I'll look for the black-hearted hussy in the Cauldron.
I may see me own hair hangin' from the belt of one of them
savages or see us bein' eaten up by octopussies, but I'll
look."

"That's my brave girl," Dylan said and got a glare and a
loud sob for his trouble.

A few minutes later, the small golden bowl was sitting
on the mess table and the girl was pouring the pink liquid
she kept for that special purpose into it. Churchward, Mr.
Asbury, Mr. H. and Dr. W. all gathered around Dylan
and Clarinda. The girl bent close over the bowl in which
the pink liquid had started to swirl, her face reflecting the
strange glow from it.

"Look into the Cauldron of Keridwen, friends, look

deep into the Cauldron," she intoned. "There are more worlds than one in Keridwen's Cauldron. See the bubbles swirling. . . . The bubbles that are the worlds stir there in the depths. See the pictures starting to form . . . pictures of the past, the future and the present."

"I say," Dr. W. said, "something is appearing in there; it's almost like a kinescope."

"A slightly different principle, I dare say," H. observed.

"Sh, don't disturb the power," Clarinda said without looking up. "The bubbles swirl and the picture forms. . . . We see a forest glade . . . a glade of mighty, sky-probing trees where the sun filters through but dimly. We see a lady, her servants and guides. They have set up camp."

"Yes," Dylan whispered, "there's a tent . . . horses grazing with a man standing guard. And there's Lady Philippa by the fire with her maid."

"So now we know she's in Tir-Narog, but just where exactly?" Churchward asked.

"Wait," Clarinda said "Keridwen will give us a sign."

Dylan studied the picture. "From the slant of the sunlight, I'd say she is in almost the same longitude as we are. Latitude is a bit more difficult to tell."

"Ah, we have another practioner of the art of deduction," H. said.

"A practitioner of the art of exploration," Dylan said. "Notice a snow-capped mountain peak over there between the two trees on the far side of the camp. That would be to the north of Lady Philippa's camp." He reached into a chart case and pulled out a map which he spread out beside the Cauldron. "They are almost certainly due north of us in this area marked *Terra Incognita*. That mountain must be part of the Drackensberrgs, part of the great central system of ranges we call the Mountains of Forever."

"Then she is near Helvitia and headed into the land of Asura," Asbury said.

"No, I think not. Asura welcomes no visitors and makes it extremely unpleasant for anyone approaching their borders," Dylan said. "We have been assuming the lady traveled up the Myrk in that steam launch. Suppose, however, that she actually headed north on the Medelgo to a place in the Prefecture of the West. It would be a simple matter to hire guides, horses and pack animals and strike out through the West Wind Pass into Tir-Narog."

"Heading for where?" H. asked.

"That's a good question," Dylan said and stuck his head out of the deckhouse to summon Gibbon and Lean Buck.

"Is there a trail leading west from West Wind Pass through Tir-Narog?" he asked the tobacco-chewing guide.

"No," Gibbon said after thinking it over for a minute, "no trail leading west 'cept for a few Skerling hunting paths not fit for horses or pack animals."

"But the lady definitely has pack animals with her," Dylan said, puzzled.

"Maybe lady not go toward setting sun," Lean Buck said without taking his admiring eyes off Clarinda's wealth of coppery hair. "Maybe take Old Deer Trail."

Dylan looked questioningly at Gibbon, who looked around for a place to spit, didn't find one and had to swallow tobacco juice before he could answer, "Runs southwest from West Wind Pass."

"But you said no when I asked you—"

"You asked me if there was a trail running west," Gibbon said. "You didn't say nothing about no trail running southwest."

Dylan tried not to show his exasperation. This was either the most literal-minded individual he had ever encountered or the stupidest.

"Where does the trail run to?" he asked, trying to phrase the question so even the bald-headed frontiersman couldn't misinterpret it. "Can you show me on the map?"

"Don't have to use no map," Gibbon said, shifting the plug from one cheek to the other. "It runs to the salt licks around Myrk Lake."

"Myrk Lake, of course!" Dylan said, striking a fist into the palm of his hand. "That's where the colony is located!"

"If that's true, this is the most brilliant piece of deduction I've ever seen," H. said.

"Yes, it is," Dylan agreed, "and it's yours."

"I beg your pardon?"

"Myrk Lake was once part of Myrk River," Dylan said. "A tremendous earthquake, back in the thirteenth century after the founding of the city, caused the course of the river to change, leaving Myrk Lake a landlocked swamp with almost exactly the same geological and floral makeup as the river. Your deduction was correct all the time; you just lacked one vital piece of information, my friend, one that I had but didn't connect."

"I say, H., extraordinary," Dr. W. said.

"Elementary, my dear W.," Mr. H. said, looking happier than he had in some time.

Lean Buck had taken a silent step toward Clarinda, who was still bent over the Cauldron, his fingers reaching for the glistening hair while his other hand drew his knife.

Dylan started around the table to intercept the youth although he was sure he intended only to cut off one curl, but despite her seeming concentration, Clarinda beat him to it.

"Listen, me lean brown bucko," she said, "if you so much as touch one hair on me head, I'll turn you into a field mouse and set an owl bigger than the moon to huntin' you down."

The Skerling's mouth fell open and he backed off a step or two.

"She can do it too, laddie," Dylan said. "She's the most powerful redheaded witch Avallon ever had."

Suddenly Clarinda screamed and threw her hands over her eyes, stumbling toward Dylan and throwing herself into his arms. Her terror obviously had nothing to do with Lean Buck's desire to snatch a sample of her hair. She was screaming because of something she had seen in the Cauldron.

"Oh, Dylan, me love, hold me!" she sobbed.

"What is it, darling, what did you see?" he asked, trying to soothe her while the others stared in surprise.

"It was terrible . . . too terrible! I didn't want to look but I had to. The *tag hairn* showed me what I didn't want to see!"

"Tell me about it," Dylan said gently.

"The bubbles swirled and the pattern changed. The glade where the woman is camped faded and I saw Avallon . . . the Avallon of the future. And I looked for all its busy bustling streets full of people and—" She burst into fresh sobs.

"And what?"

"There were none! No people, no life in all that great city! Only the black dust left by the Martian gas and the red weed they brought with them from Thor. That ugly red weed seemed to cover all of the land and beyond."

"My God!" Dr. W. gasped. "The red weed. It did grow all over the part of England they conquered. It died out after they were destroyed."

"It was a true future," Clarinda sobbed. "The Cauldron never lies."

"But, darling, you told me yourself that the future is fan-shaped and so what you saw isn't—"

"There was something else," she said, trembling like a leaf in a gale, "something even more terrible. I looked for you and me, love, and we wasn't!"

Chapter 12

An overland expedition was organized the next morning to head for the Old Deer Trail and cut Lady Philippa off before she could reach Myrk Lake. The reasoning behind this strategy was that if she could be kept from joining the others at the secret base, it might work against the plans of the Circle of Life. There was also the possibility that the lady might be prevailed upon to change sides or at least provide needed information about plans and arrangements for the Martian landings.

"I hear the Skerlings have interestin' ways of makin' people talk who don't want to," Clarinda said as she watched Dylan and the other men pack supplies and ammunition for the overland trek. "One little trick is to—"

"It's just as well you're remaining on the ship," Dylan interrupted.

"I'm doin' no such thing!" she said. "You dragged me this far against me will and you're not goin' to leave me pinin' away on this sinkin' boat until the octopussies come to gobble me up. I seen us dead, love, and you're not goin' to be dead in one place and me in another."

When they were ready to leave, Dylan spoke to Asbury and the officer in charge of the volunteers. "Once we reach Old Deer Trail, we'll send a runner back with the news."

"Yes, sir. Then what?" asked the young Imperial Marine in mufti who commanded the former sappers and miners.

"A forced march," Dylan said. "Strike as quickly as you

can across country and go directly to Myrk Lake. You'll have Lean Buck and his father to guide you. If the Martians haven't landed yet, we'll seize the Circle of Life base, lay mines and prepare to attack them on landing. If they have already landed, we'll send runners to St. Rory to call down the *Vengeance* and *Flying Cloud* and attack with everything at once."

"And if the Martians are out of their capsules and into their battle machines?" Churchward asked.

"Then we'll attack anyway, do what we can and—"

"And die," Mr. H. finished grimly.

The expedition started out with Gibbon and two Skerlings leading the way. Dylan and the three Earthmen followed, carrying heavy packs loaded with dynamite charges and extra ammo for the high-powered rifles they carried. Clarinda trailed after Dylan carrying a duffle bag holding her cauldron and a few bottles of things she thought might possibly be useful, like eye of newt, snake powder and elixir of love.

"Maybe we could slip a little of Keridwen's own formula into their drinkin' water," she suggested. "If them octopussies got busy makin' love with each other, they might not have time to eat people."

"Ahem," Dr. W. said with an embarrassed cough, "but I'm afraid the Martians are . . . well, unisexual."

"They're what?" Clarinda asked.

"There is only one sex among them," the doctor explained. "When they are ready to reproduce, which is only once in a lifetime, I believe, they simply, ahem, bud."

"Why, I never!" Clarinda said, properly scandalized. "The filthy things!"

Long-Arm Gibbon managed to get the expedition lost twice, the second time so thoroughly that they found they had doubled back in their tracks and were standing on the banks of the Myrk River again. They had lost two full days when Dylan decided to take over. At the very least he was capable of judging general directions even in the dense woods.

After a difficult three-day tramp through tangled underbrush and swampy ground, they came to the Old Deer Trail. Then came the problem of learning whether Lady Philippa and her guides had passed that way. Long-Arm Gibbon could find no sign of their passing, but the two Skerlings did. They would only talk to Clarinda, for some reason, though.

"They say that the lady and her guides are only a few hours ahead of us," she reported. "They're thinkin' that when the fightin' starts, they're goin' to grab me and run for it. For which I am placin' a geas on them that will turn their hair to snakes and make their feet go so flat they can hardly walk."

"Hold off on the geas until we don't need them any longer," Dylan said in her ear. "I'd hate to be lost in these woods with only that super-scout veteran Skerling tracker, Long-Arm Gibbon, to show me the way."

"I'll keep it in reserve then, like me old man does his right while he's jabbin' with his left," Clarinda said, "but just so they remember their manners, I'll give them a couple of jabs."

The younger of the two Skerlings had been sitting on his haunches nearby. Suddenly he leaped almost five feet into the air and started beating at something under his loincloth. The other one, who had been leaning against a tree picking his teeth with a knife, let out a yelp and began slapping at a large black bat that was tangled in his hair.

"There, that'll teach you not to squat over a nest of red ants or stand under a bat's nest!"

"Bats don't nest in trees," Dylan said.

"They do if I tell 'em to," Clarinda said.

Dylan laughed, thinking that of late Clarinda's power seemed to be increasing. At one time her spells and geas had been a chancy thing, a wild talent, but now she seemed able almost to turn it on and off at will.

"Maybe it has somethin' to do with me reachin' puberty," she suggested, reading his mind again.

"Puberty? You're long past that stage."

"How do you know how long it takes for the priestess of a love cult to grow up?"

She was joking, of course, but Dylan was still intrigued by the seeming increase in her talents. He had no time to think about it at the moment, however, or to wonder what it would mean to their future relationship.

They overtook Lady Philippa's party two hours later. The pair of hired guides were armed, but when confronted by twice their number of determined men they quickly threw down their rifles and surrendered. Lady Philippa and her butler reacted differently.

The butler, a husky balding man in his early forties, pulled a forty-four revolver from a haversack and brought it up quickly to snap off a shot that sent splinters flying from a tree right beside Dylan's ear. Mr. H. snapped off two shots in return and the man collapsed across a log and lay still. By that time, Lady Philippa's small pearl-handled revolver was aimed steadily at a point between Dylan's eyes. Her finger was tightening on the trigger when Clarinda struck her from the side in a flying tackle and sent her sprawling.

"Take your hands off me!" Philippa ordered as the redhead dragged her to her feet. "What is the meaning of this? How dare you!"

"Stow it, you little bustle-twitcher, or I'll give you a taste of me fist," Clarinda said, shoving her ladyship toward Dylan.

"Mr. MacBride, what is the meaning of this outrage?" Lady Philippa demanded.

"I think you already know," Dylan said. "We are armed and have come to stop the Martian invasion. If Circle of Life members get in the way, they will have to suffer the consequences."

Lady Philippa glanced around at the group and laughed. "An army of four men and a girl, with a couple of skulking Indians and whatever that other strange-looking creature is. Do you honestly think you can hold back the forces of destiny?"

"Even the forces of destiny are subject to alteration if caught in their cradle," Mr. H. said.

"The Martians are coming and they will conquer," the woman said as though repeating a basic law of nature. "Nothing you can do will prevent it."

"Well, maybe you won't be around to greet 'em, me fine lady."

"It doesn't matter," Lady Philippa said. "What matters is that the superior race will survive."

"The dustbin of history is filled with the pretensions of others who thought themselves superior," Dylan said. "Now, where are your friends?"

"Where you'll never find them!" Philippa said. "I would be with them by now if I hadn't stayed behind to throw you off the scent and if the Martian flyer hadn't developed problems when it was supposed to pick me up."

Dylan exchanged a glance with Mr. H. That bit of information was welcome. Things would be a little easier for them with the flying machine out of commission.

"The base can't be too far from here," Dylan said. "Why don't we split up into groups of two and search for it?"

"Or maybe it would be better to send Gibbon and the Skerlings to find it," Churchward suggested. "That way we keep our forces concentrated for attack or defense."

Dylan didn't trust Gibbon to do anything right, but the others seemed to favor the latter plan, so he reluctantly agreed to it.

"I'll find them people for you, Mr. MacBride," the scout assured Dylan. "You couldn't hide a needle in this country that Long-Arm Gibbon couldn't find."

"Just find the hidden base," Clarinda said. "Never mind the needle; we're not goin' to be doin' any sewin'."

"Don't worry, missy, I'll find 'em," Gibbon said as he and the two natives headed west along the trail.

It was five hours before he returned but he had done what he'd promised and more. He had found the Circle of Life base and brought the members back with him . . . all twenty of them and all armed.

"What the devil!" Dylan yelled as the woods around them were suddenly alive with armed men and Koot Hoomi, Professor Philander and a man in the turned collar of a clergyman were coming along the trail toward them.

"You'll do well to throw down your weapons, gentlemen," Koot Hoomi said. "You are surrounded and I assure you we will not hesitate to kill you if you resist."

"How did you know where we were?" Mr. H. asked when he had tossed his rifle and revolver onto the small heap of weapons his companions were also contributing to.

Professor Philander smiled thinly. "The tobacco-chewing gentleman in the buckskin jacket offered to bring us to you and we accepted. He was most helpful."

Dylan looked at Gibbon. "Why? *Why?*"

"Well, I allowed as how you was so eager to find these folks, and they wanted to see you too, so I figured I'd make it easier all 'round by bringin' 'em along back here to meet you. Wasn't that the right thing to do?"

Dylan didn't bother to answer as he tossed his weapons on top of the others. The man was hopeless.

"Mr. Gibbon, if you'll place your rifle and knife there too, we can be on our way back to the base," Philander said.

"You want me to give up my shootin' iron?" Long-Arm asked. "How come?"

"To tell you the truth, sir, I'm afraid you might shoot yourself with it."

"Now this is a fine kettle of fish you got us into!" Clarinda whispered fiercely to Dylan as they were led down the trail by their captors. "I suppose you're expectin' me to get us out."

"I'm not sure anything can get us out," Dylan said.

"Nothing can," Lady Philippa said from behind them. "The Martian capsules arrive this afternoon and the conquest of mankind begins."

Myrk Lake was only a few miles further along the trail and they arrived there before noon. The base wasn't as large as Dylan had expected and there was an air of impermanence about it since it consisted mostly of tents with only a few scattered log cabins and sheds. It was, however, well disguised against discovery from the air. The buildings and tents were shielded by the branches of large spreading trees and even the flying machine poised on the bank of the lake had branches piled over it to prevent detection.

"What was the point in dragging them all back here?" Angel Annie asked Koot Hoomi as Dylan and the others were herded into a windowless log cabin. "Why didn't you finish them off where you found them?"

Koot Hoomi smiled at her indulgently. "Think about it, my dear. Our guests will have come a long way and may be short on rations."

The woman nodded. "But wouldn't they be just as valuable dead? It makes me nervous having them around."

Dean Matthews, the clergyman, spoke up. "My dear, if you were an honored guest and a feast was being prepared for you, wouldn't you want the food kept fresh? That's what we're doing, keeping it fresh by keeping it on the hoof, so to speak."

"Why, you old devil!" Clarinda yelled. "You with you turned collar and your look of butter not meltin' in your mouth, you're perfectly willin' to serve us up as supper to a bunch of cold-blooded monsters!"

The clergyman turned his cherubic smile on the priestess. "From your point of view, my dear, I understand why you might object, but if you consider it calmly, with a little prayerful thought, you'll come to understand what an honor it will be for you to become part of a being nobler and better than yourself."

"Ha!" Clarinda snorted. "There'll never be a day when a slimy squid is better than a MacTague . . . or a MacBride either! You call yourself a man of God but you're nothin' but a common murderer!"

"It is because I am a man of God that I recognize His will. The Martians are the master race, and it is God's will that we serve them. To oppose them would be to fall into mortal sin."

"Enough of this pointless chatter," Koot Hoomi said. "Tie their wrists and ankles and lock them in the cabin. We still have work to do before the first capsule arrives."

Dylan, Clarinda, Gibbon and the three Earthmen were bound tightly with whipcord line and shoved into the almost total darkness of the cabin. Dylan sank down on the dirt floor with his back against the wall, trying to resist the despair that was closing in on him.

"Dylan, love," Clarinda said from close beside him, "don't be feelin' so bad. I wasn't doin' all that yellin' and cater-waulin' for nothin', you know."

"Why were you doing it? Surely you didn't think you could change their minds?"

"Ha! You might as well try to make the multiplication tables come out different as to make that crew into human bein's," she said. "I made all that noise to cover the fact that I managed to slip a knife out of one of them fellow's pockets with the power and hide it in me boot top."

"Bully for you, Miss Clarinda!" Churchward said. "But was there any need for that when you can use your power now to untie us all?"

"And unlock the door also, I'll wager," Dr. W. said.

"Don't bet more than you're willin' to lose," Clarinda said, " 'cause I think they got me stymied."

"You mean you've lost the power?" Dylan asked in dismay.

"No, I still got it, but there's a counterforce, a blocking geas, you might call it. I tried to give that bloodthirsty preacher a squeeze around his fat neck with his own collar but nothing happened. Then I tried to trip that Angel Annie on her double chin but all she did was waddle a little more. Koot Hoomi's turban wouldn't pull down over his eyes either.

Each time I tried, I felt another force resisting mine."

"Well, I guess that finishes us," Churchward said despondently. "What a fate."

"Well, at least the Skerlings got away," Dr. W. said. "Perhaps they'll make their way back to the *Thunderbolt* and bring Asbury and the men."

"Don't expect they will," Gibbon said. "After we found them people you was lookin' for, I figured we didn't need 'em no more so I told 'em they could go home."

"I keep getting this feeling," Dylan said, "that the one way to save the human race would be to enlist Long-Arm Gibbon on the side of the Martians."

"Well, we still got me knife," Clarinda said. "If you'll be reachin' it out of me boot, love, we'll cut ourselves loose."

"An untold number of Martians are hurtling toward Annwn equipped with weapons of unparalleled power and all we have is a knife," Mr. H. said. "Somehow the odds seem a little long."

"But they did bring our weapons and the packs with the dynamite into the camp," Dylan said. "I saw them being put in the shed near where the flying machine is hidden."

Dr. W.'s usually cheerful voice was doleful as he said, "So all we have to do is cut ourselves loose, find a way to break out of this cabin, fight our way through twenty armed men and get our weapons back."

"Probably just in time to get ourselves burned to cinders by Martian heat-rays," Churchward added.

Dylan had moved closer to Clarinda, searching for the knife in the top of her boot with his bound hands. He pushed aside one petticoat and then another and felt around with his fingers. What he felt was firm, round flesh.

"That's me calf," Clarinda said.

"Yes," Dylan said and moved his hand quickly.

"And that's me thigh."

"I'm sorry, I didn't mean—"

"Nobody's objectin', 'cept it don't seem like the time nor the place," she said, laughing.

Moving his hand in the opposite direction, he located the top of her boot and worked his fingers around the handle of the knife.

"Got it," he said. "Now help me find your hands." He felt her wriggle against him warmly and then her hands met his. That was when it got hard. He had to feel around her wrists with his fingertips without dropping the knife and find a place to cut the cord without cutting her.

"Easy does it," he said, sliding his fingers over the backs of her hands to the beginning of the cord. Sweat formed on his forehead even in the chilly darkness as he changed the knife to his other hand and turned the blade against the cord. The knife was sharp and in a minute the girl's hands were free. It was only a matter of seconds then for her to take the knife, cut the bonds on her ankles and free him.

"Now, let's see what we can do with the door," Dylan said, getting to his feet while Clarinda cut the others loose.

"Maybe I can help," Mr. H. said, coming to his side. "I've had quite a bit of experience picking locks in my time."

"I'm afraid this isn't the kind of lock you mean," Dylan said, looking out through a crack between the logs. "The door is bolted on the outside with a large two-by-four fitted across it in twin brackets."

"Hopeless," H. said. "They must have intended this for a prison from the beginning . . . no windows and barred from the outside."

"We still have the knife," Dylan said. "Maybe we can cut our way out."

"Yes, *if* the blade doesn't break, we might be able to do it in several days, *if* we have several days."

There was a sound like that of a dozen express trains, a roar that seemed to shake the very foundations of the earth beneath them. It was followed by a light so intense that it lit up the inside of the windowless cabin just by filtering through the cracks.

The prisoners stared at each other's pale faces in the unexpected brightness.

"The Martians are landing," Mr. H. said. "We'll feel the impact of the first capsule in a—"

His words were cut off by an exposion that rocked the building and caused the dust to rise from the floor and dance in the eerie light.

"If we had only had the time," Churchward said despairingly as they were plummeted into darkness again. "If we had only had the time."

Chapter 13

"Perhaps we're not finished yet," Dr. W. said an hour or so later as Dylan worked frantically with the knife to cut a hole large enough for a hand to reach through to the heavy bar across the door. "I seem to remember there was a considerable period between the landing of the first Martian capsule and the time it opened up."

"Yes," H. said, "twelve hours and thirty-seven minutes precisely. The time it took for the outside of the capsule to cool sufficiently from the heating caused by its passage through the atmosphere."

"Can you cut a big enough hole in eight hours?" Churchward asked Dylan.

"More like eight hours plus two weeks," Dylan said, feeling with his fingers the tiny hole he had managed to bore in the thick log.

"I have a feelin' that we're not goin' to be gettin' any two weeks," Clarinda said. "Them beasties are goin' to be powerful hungry comin' fifty million miles to supper."

"Let me spell you with the knife," Long-Arm Gibbon said. "I used to be an expert whittler."

"I think I'd rather get blisters," Dylan said, thinking that the only thing worse than being trapped in this cabin with only a knife would be to be trapped there without one after Gibbon had broken the blade or dropped it through to the outside.

"I still can't help you," Clarinda said. "I've been tryin' to lift that bar with the power but someone else is sittin' on top of it holdin' it down with the power and I can't budge it."

"I think we have to face the fact that several members of the Circle of Life have developed powers of the mind since coming to Annwn," Mr H. said. "There seems to be a magical —at least a mystical—influence on this planet that doesn't exist on Earth. I am inclined to think that the natural laws of the two planets are different and that here on Annwn the powers of the mind are part of those natural laws."

"If they have developed powers of the mind, why haven't we?" Churchward asked. "I've been here almost three years and I can't even read something simple, like the mind of Mr. Gibbon."

"I suspect there has to be a predisposition toward it to start with," H. said, "and all of the Circle of Life people have been dabbling in the occult, sampling esoteric cults and mystical beliefs. Previously, they only thought they had magical powers; now some of them actually do."

"Than we're losing even the advantage of Clarinda's power," Dylan said. "Weren't the odds long enough before?"

"Maybe something will happen, maybe we'll get a break of some kind and—" Churchward's words were drowned out in a repetition of the express train roar and the dazzling light.

"Sure now, somethin' is happenin', but it isn't a break for us," Clarinda said. "Another of them bloody things is landin'."

"They're coming in mighty fast," H. said as the sound of the capsule's impact died away. "Much faster than during their descent on England."

"They must be hungrier," Clarinda said. "Oh, Keridwen, me darling, you're going to be one lonely goddess when Clarinda's in the belly of an octopussy from Mars or Thor or wherever."

"That's it, Clarinda, that's it!" Dylan said. "Call on Keridwen! Ask her to lift that bar, ask her to set us free."

"Oh, now, I wouldn't be knowin' about that," Clarinda said. "It seems like a menial kind of task for a lady goddess to be liftin' bars and all that."

"Tell her how important it is!" Mr. H. said emphatically.

"Tell her if she wants any worshipers left, she better lend a hand," Dylan said.

"She hasn't got all that many that it would matter to her," Clarinda said. "Love cults have gone out of style, what with women wearin' bloomers and bobbin' their hair and all."

"Try, please try!"

"What do you think I'm doin'? I'm callin' and callin' her! Just 'cause I'm not callin' out loud doesn't mean I'm not yellin' bloody murder in me mind."

"Any luck yet?" Churchward asked the girl an hour later.

"Nothin'! The cosmic connection must be on the blink. The wire in me mind isn't rattlin' in hers or she's not answering if it does," Clarinda said disconsolately.

"Keep trying, darling," Dylan said, putting his arm around her. He had given up his place at the hole in the log to Dr. W., who was chipping away without thought for his surgeon's hands.

"I am, I'm strainin' a psychic ligament, but there's no answer. Sometimes I think Keridwen must have disconnected her end of the line, or maybe she's got more important things to do."

"How much time have we?" Dr. W., who had been relieved at the hole by Mr. H., asked as he stretched in the semi-light of a new day.

"Two hours, I make it," Churchward said. "It's been a little over ten hours since the first capsule landed."

"And we've counted ten more coming in since then," Dylan said. "Damn it, we should already be attacking them —and here we sit, helpless! Keep after Keridwen, darling. Let me have a turn with that knife, old chap."

Feeling the size of the hole, Dylan felt sick at heart because it was still so small. "This must be iron wood."

"Mahogany, I believe," H. said, lowering his long, lanky body to the floor wearily.

"It's gettin' lighter," Gibbon said. "That crack must be gettin' some bigger."

"It's almost daylight," H. said, dryly. "The first light of the last days of the human race, I should judge."

"I can't reach her! Dylan, I can't find her," Clarinda sobbed against Dylan's shoulder. "I keep thinkin' that I'm touchin' her but then she isn't there."

"Listen! What's that sound?" Churchward had his ear to the door. "There's something on the other side of the door. The bar is being lifted, I think!"

"Yes, someone or something is lifting the bar! Thank God! Thank Keridwen!" Dylan said, his eye against the peep hole.

"No, it couldn't be me darlin' goddess. I never reached her!"

The door swung open and not Keridwen but Lady Philippa stood there outlined against the quickening light of dawn.

"Dylan, I had to come. I couldn't let them kill you," the Earth woman said. "Hurry! You've only got a few minutes before they come to get you."

"Is it Dylan then that you're worried about?" Clarinda asked, her voice a suspicious purr.

Dylan was suspicious, too, despite the fact that the door blocking their escape now stood open. "What are you doing here?" he demanded.

"I thought I could let them kill you," Philippa said. "I was sure my mind ruled my heart but somehow it doesn't. I had a dream, a strange dream when I didn't even know I was asleep, and when it was over I knew I couldn't live if you were dead."

"Oh glory!" Clarinda said. "She did it! Me darlin' goddess did it, but why this way?"

"I had to set you free, Dylan." Philippa's hands were clinging to Dylan's and he didn't know whether to push her away or accept what she had done. "The Circle of Life was going to sacrifice you. You must leave at once!"

"I hope that includes the rest of us as well," Mr. H. said, unrolling like a scroll as he got to his feet.

"Yes, of course," Philippa said. "That dream was so real, I had to come."

"Did you hear that?" Clarinda whispered fiercely in Dylan's ear. "That hussy of a goddess of mine did it! She wouldn't deign to lift that bar with her own lily-white hands so she sent this one to do it. But why did she have to make the woman fall in love with you to accomplish it?"

"There are horses in the stable," Philippa said. "You can get away easily while the others are in the Concentration Room communicating with the Martians."

Dylan shook his head. "No. You and Clarinda take the horses and ride for it. I'm staying and I think the other men will too."

"Yes, we came here to stop the Martians, not to save our own hides," Churchward said.

"There is no question of my leaving," H. said, "and Dr. W. has never yet failed to back me in a tight situation."

"I'll go along with the ladies and take care of them," Long-Arm said.

"Not this lady, you won't!" Clarinda said. "I'd sooner trust meself in the woods to a one-eyed, one-armed steeplejack with the D.T.'s than you. Besides, I'm not leavin' Dylan."

"You can't stay, you fools! I freed you to save Dylan's life! But I won't stand by and let you wreck our plans for serving the Martians. Surely you don't think I'd betray my friends."

"Sure, and I think you would," Clarinda said with a trace of pity in her voice. "You've been bit by one of Keridwen's bugs. You've had the MacBride curse laid on your head, lassie, and you'll probably suffer from it the rest of you life just like me. There's no way you'll let Dylan be killed, and you can't kill the rest of us without killin' him."

"I . . . I don't know what you're talking about," Philippa said.

"Don't you now? Then scream for your friends," Clarinda said. "*If* you can; if the goddess will let you."

Lady Philippa opened her mouth to scream and Dylan took a quick step toward her, intending to stifle it, but the sound never came out. Her vocal cords were straining, lips and tongue ready to produce a piercing yell, but nothing happened. After a few minutes, she gave up. "It goes against everything I believe in, but I guess I can't if it means betraying Dylan."

"All right," Dylan said, taking charge. "Clarinda, take Lady Philippa and go in the woods and hide. The rest of us will go get our supplies and locate the Martian capsules."

"And then what?" Philippa asked.

"We'll destroy them, if we can," Dylan said.

"No! You don't understand! Please, you mustn't. Dylan, you mustn't." Philippa tried to cling to him.

"Clarinda, take her into the woods and make sure she stays there," Dylan said. "Put a geas on her if you have to."

"Come on, me fancy lady," Clarinda said, taking hold of Philippa's arm, "You and me be going to pick a few daisies while these bully boys go get themselves killed, like as not."

Dylan brushed his lips against the redhead's cheek, then he and the three Earthmen took off at a run toward the shed where he had seen their gear and arms deposited.

"I don't see any sign of the Martian capsules but they must be somewhere nearby," Dylan said.

"Look! Over there in that low-lying grassy area near the lake, I think I see a glow." Churchward was pointing toward the extensive salt flats.

"Yes, it makes sense," H. said. "The salt flats would make

a good impact area for the capsules. They wouldn't be risking damage as they would on firmer earth."

"But wouldn't they sink in too far?" Dylan asked. They had reached the shed and he was prying open the door.

"The Circle of Life people must have tested the depth of the soft earth and found it satisfactory, because I think I see the glow of two more capsules beyond the first," H. said.

"And here comes another of the bloody things," Churchward shouted, pointing toward the southern horizon as a streaming fireball crashed across the sky and plunged into the shadowy marshes further up the shores of the lake, throwing up a huge tower of water, mud and swamp grass.

"There is another advantage to their using the salt marshes," H. said. "The capsules which landed on the commons in England started huge grass fires which interfered with the Martians' emerging from their craft. They won't have that problem here."

"All the more reason to hurry," Dylan said, forcing the door open and handing out arms and packs to the others.

"Dylan . . . Dylan, me love!" It was Clarinda, running toward them dragging a protesting Philippa along behind her. "Dylan, the first capsule is getting ready to open!"

"How do you know?" Dylan asked. "Has your power come back?"

"Not all of it, but I had me a peek and the Circle of Life boys are leavin' their Communal Room and goin' toward where the first capsule fell."

"Then we haven't much time," Dylan said. "You girls get back in the woods."

Clarinda shook her head stubbornly. "No use to it," she said. "They'd just hunt us down after they kill the rest of you anyway. I'd rather die with you than with this caterwauling female."

"Where's Gibbon?" Churchward asked.

"He took off up the trail like the Yath Hounds themselves were on his heels," Clarinda said. "Now I know why they call 'em woods runners, 'cause all he seems to do well is run away."

"Where's the first capsule down?" Dylan demanded of Lady Philippa, but she shook her head and turned away.

"It's that one," Clarinda said, "the one where the glow is brightest. I had me a little peek look and there they come, the whole bloody traitor crew of em headin' toward it."

She was right. The members of the Circle of Life were parading solemnly toward the salt marshes carrying what looked to be presents and sacrificial offerings for their tentacled gods. Dean Matthews, dressed in the full regalia of the Church of England, Koot Hoomi in a jeweled turban, Angel Annie in her purple robe, and Professor Philander in mortarboard and academic robe led some twenty others toward the glowing area in the marshes.

"They haven't seen us yet," H. said. "They seem to be in some state of spiritual ecstasy where only the meeting with their gods is important to them. If we stay low and follow them, they'll never notice us until it's too late."

"Be ready with your rifles and dymanite charges," Dylan said.

"They go to welcome our masters," Lady Philippa said. "I should be with them."

"You'll stay right with us, me lady dove," Clarinda told her, "or I'll be turnin' you into a bedbug and stepping on you."

Clarinda was quite capable of handling Lady Philippa, Dylan noted with a grin. He wouldn't have to keep an eye on her himself.

Dylan led the others through the hip-high swamp grass, partially sinking into the water and mud, but easily keeping the Circle of Life members in sight without being seen. The fanatics' eyes and probably their thoughts were totally concentrated on the circular mound of dirt ahead of them where the first capsule rested in a crater.

"We'll split up, circle the thing and attack from both sides," Dylan directed. "Take advantage of cover as much as possible and remember that once the heat-ray gets into action we won't stand a chance."

As the members of the Circle of Life reached the mound around the crater and began to climb it, Dylan, Churchward, Clarinda and Lady Philippa separated from the famous consulting detective and his cohort. H. and Dr. W. went to the north side of the crater and Dylan and Churchward to the south side with Clarinda yanking the protesting Philippa along through the mud.

"I wish I had me full power," Clarinda was saying. "I'd scare us up a mist that even a Martian couldn't see through."

"We'll have to do the best we can with natural cover," Dylan said, crawling up the mound with the others close behind. Lying on his belly and peeking over the edge so as to remain unobserved, he saw his first Martian capsule.

"Yes, it's exactly as Wells described it," he said to Churchward and Clarinda, who had scrambled up to lie beside him with Philippa still in tow. The Thing, as Wells had referred to it, was almost completely buried in the black mud. The part that showed looked like a huge cylinder, its outline softened by thick, scaly, dun-colored incrustations. To Dylan's trained eye, it looked to be at least the thirty yards across that Wells had estimated.

"It isn't glowing any more," Churchward whispered. "It must be cool enough for the hatch to be opening."

"It is. Look there where the crust is falling off and you can see the hatch turning."

"Just like in the book," Churchward said. "And also like in the book, there is an Earth delegation waiting to greet the aliens in peace."

"But another Earth-Annwn delegation is waiting to give them a more deserved welcome," Dylan added, taking a cigar from the pack he carried and lighting it. He hated cigars but a good hot glow on the end made a reliable slow match to light the fuses of the dynamite-stick bombs. Then he put his pack down on the embankment and took out one of the bombs. "We're too late to do as we planned and plant charges under this capsule. We're going to have to try to throw them through the hatch as soon as it's open."

"Would you murder them without even letting them speak to you?" Lady Philippa asked.

"I sure would," Dylan answered, "if I get a chance."

"I think the capsule is almost open," Churchward said. He also had a cigar in his mouth and was holding four sticks of dynamite tied together. "Shall we throw as soon as the lid falls away?"

"No, wait a few moments. Let the things start to crawl out. Let them see the Circle of Light gang waiting for them and feel safe, then throw with all your might right into the open hatch."

Over a foot of shining screw was visible now and it was rocking in the housing as though about to fall.

The Circle of Life members raised a chant of welcome.

Dean Matthews with cross raised on high, Koot Hoomi with an olive branch and Angel Annie with a crystal ball moved down the inner side of the crater toward the opening. As the lid fell away the worshipers shouted and sang with joy.

"Welcome. Welcome, noble ones. Welcome, great beings from space. Your people await your will," Koot Hoomi shouted.

"We swoon at your feet," Angel Annie, her double chins quivering with joy, shouted. "We bask in the spiritual light from your beings."

"Your intellects will stun us, your spirituality will shame us and your . . ." Professor Philander paused in mid-sentence as something slid from the hatch of the capsule. It wasn't a Martian as everyone had expected but a black, cameralike affair.

"That's the heat-ray!" Dylan said, too stunned to react at once. "They didn't wait until they were out of the capsule to—"

Lady Philippa screamed as a sudden flash of light and a mass of greenish smoke came out of the capsule followed by a long, loud, droning noise. A ghostly beam of light flickered from the camera and became actual flame as it leaped out, first at the leading members of the Council of Life who were in the pit bowing in worship and then at those who crowded the brim of the pit bowing in worship.

It was as though each man and woman had suddenly been touched by some cosmic torch as the heat-ray leaped among them.

"They're killing them! Oh, God, they're killing their friends." Lady Philippa sobbed, trying to break away from Clarinda to run toward the flaming members of the Circle of Life.

"Now! Now, Churchward!" Dylan shouted to make himself heard over the hissing ray and the screams of the dying. "Throw the bombs!"

Even as he spoke, he lit the fuse and hurled his dynamite bomb at the open hatchway of the capsule. He cursed furiously as he saw it strike the metal coping and bounce away to lay with fuse burning a few feet from the open hatch.

Two other bombs came hurtling from the other side of the pit. One passed over the capsule and fell into the pit and the other fell short. "Damn it . . . all missed! Damn it to hell!" Dylan swore. Sighting along his rifle, he began to throw steel-jacketed slugs at a grayish thing that was pushing its way out of the capsule with the camera of the heat-ray held in two tentacles. He could see the slugs striking home but without much effect. The heat-ray was swinging toward him.

Then Churchward threw his bomb with the fuse burning very short. The bomb seemed to drift lazily through the air toward the opening in which the camera was slowly swinging. For a minute Dylan thought that it also would miss but then he was yelling crazily in joy as he saw it go crashing right into the opening.

All four bombs went off at the same moment, throwing Dylan back down the slope of the pit and sending Lady Philippa sprawling after him.

"Right in the catcher's glove, so to speak," Churchward said as he lay covering his head as the whole pit seemed to erupt into the sky and come raining down on their heads.

"You got it! You got it!" It sounded like Dr. W. yelling from the other side of the pit.

Dylan dragged himself back up to the top of the pit and silently stared down at the shattered opening of the Martian capsule.

"The power is back!" Clarinda was shouting to him. "As soon as those bloody beasties wiped out the Circle of Life, I had it all back!"

"They're dead . . . all dead. So much love. So much hope and spiritual beauty, all gone. Murdered in cold blood by those they worshiped!" Lady Philippa was staring with sick eyes at the charred bodies of her friends in the pit and scattered along its rim. "Why did they kill the people who only wished to worship them?"

"I have a feeling that you overestimated their spiritual and moral natures," Dylan said, "and didn't pay enough attention to their previous actions on Earth."

"Dylan, the other capsules are opening fast!" Clarinda said. "Several of them are almost open."

"Let's go," Dylan shouted, grabbing up the haversack with the rest of his bombs in it. "Clarinda, stay with Philippa and—"

"No!" the Earth girl said. "I want to help now. I must help!"

"She means it," Clarinda said. "Besides, I'm going along. I'm going to work you up a mist that'll let you get right on top of them, even if the ray is in action."

"It'll help," Dylan said. "I thought we'd have more time while they crawled out and set up the heat-ray like they did on Earth, but now they come out shooting."

"That's why we've got to get close enough to ram a charge right down their throats as soon as the capsule opens," H. said. "Come on, gentlemen, ladies, let's go!"

The four men, with the two girls following close behind and Clarinda mumbling a spell as she ran, started toward the next Martian capsule on the run.

"Charge, gentlemen!" Dr. W. shouted, waving his revolver over his head. "Charge, in the name of God and the Queen!"

Chapter 14

There were already at least eight Martian capsules down in the salt marshes around Myrk Lake. Even as the small band of adventurers moved on to their next target, the sky lightened and the earth rocked with the thunderous passage of yet another across the sky.

"Can we ever stop them?" Churchward asked. "They're coming in so fast I don't see how we can—"

"We've got to keep trying," Dylan said as they dashed toward the nearest pit, from which the glow of overheated metal had faded and the sound of metal screeching on metal could be heard.

"It's opening!" H. shouted. "Remember, they have to be stopped before they can get out. Once even one of them gets into its battle machine, only a battery of masked guns or a large warship has the slightest chance against it."

"Stand by!" Dylan instructed as they reached the edge of the crater of mud and grass around the second capsule. "The lid is about to come off. Have your bombs ready and throw them before they can open fire with the ray camera."

The four men waited, each with a cigar in his mouth and a dynamite bomb in his hand, while the two girls crouched down behind the embankment holding extra bombs to hand up.

"Churchward, you throw first," Dylan said. "If you make a direct hit, we might be able to save the other bombs."

As the lid of the hatch wobbled and fell away, Churchward lit the fuse of his bomb. A big, round, grayish bulk about the size of a bear was dragging itself painfully in the increased gravity toward the opening of the capsule. Behind it loomed another gray bulk and that one held the camera-like mechanism of the heat-ray.

"Now, Churchward! Fod God's sake, now!" H. shouted as they all stood stunned by their first clear view of the monstrous enemy.

The sound of H.'s voice caused signs of agitation among the Martians, and the camera device was passed rapidly from tentacle to tentacle as the second alien handed it to the first.

Churchward's bomb sailed through the air, tumbling end over end toward its target, an opening about three feet wide. There was a sudden blinding explosion that knocked Churchward, H. and Dr. W. off their feet. The bomb had gone off within a few feet of the opening of the capsule.

Somehow keeping his footing, Dylan could see the lead Martian crumpled in the entryway, black blood oozing from its wounds. As the black smoke cleared, the second Martian was again reaching for the camera gun and lifting it slowly in one injured and one sound tentacle to aim it at them.

"Down, everybody, down!" Dylan yelled and, lighting his bomb as the alien weapon began to smoke, he threw it directly at the creature there in the entrance. Then he hurled himself down the embankment, dragging Clarinda with him as death licked out across the crater toward them.

The heat was unbearable as the very air above them seemed to turn to fire. The three Earthmen had leaped for cover at almost the same instant as Dylan and the four men and two girls crouched behind the ring of mud and weeds, watching the heat-ray surge back and forth over their heads until the thunder of another dynamite explosion nearly deafened them.

"Did I get it? the heat-ray has stopped." Dylan wanted

to crawl back up the ridge and have a look but he didn't want to step into fiery death if the ray was still in action.

"What we need now is the periscope from the *Thunderbolt*."

"Dylan, there's another capsule opening up," Clarinda said. "I can feel the screw turning and I can sense them things crawlin' up the tunnel."

"If we make a move from behind this embankment, we may be through anyway," Dylan said, crawling up the embankment toward the ridge. "I'll have to risk a look."

Another fireball streaked across the sky, shattering the tops of several trees as it passed about three thousand yards to the south and fell with earth-quaking force into the swamp grass.

Trying to get an eye over the rim of the crater without exposing himself was hopeless, so Dylan gave up the idea of concealment and leaped to his feet for a quick look before ducking back down. Two crumpled gray blobs lay in the tunnel exit, but Dylan thought he saw movement deeper down in the capsule, as though other Martians were busy at work, perhaps getting another heat camera ready to replace the one that lay shattered between the dead aliens.

"There's still life in that capsule," he told the others. "We've got to get another bomb further down inside it."

"The next capsule is almost open," Clarinda reported.

"The rest of you go after that one," Dylan said, picking up his rifle. "I'll finish this one off."

"I say, old boy," Dr. W. commented as he scrambled away, "this is hardly the time for a bayonet charge."

"Stay here," Dylan told Clarinda, starting to clamber down the inside of the crater while the other three men headed for the third capsule. "Stay here and throw me a bomb when I'm ready for it. I want to get a closer look into that thing and see what they're doing. I'm also going to see how many slugs one of those monsters can absorb."

"Begorra, do you hear that, Keridwen?" Clarinda moaned. "Do you hear this idiot man? He'll be wantin' to hand-wrestle one of them ugly things next!"

Dylan had reached the base of the capsule and was inching toward the open hatch on his hands and knees. From deep inside the craft he could hear the whirring of machinery and a peculiar thick cry that he thought must be the Martians' means of vocal communication.

There was still a great deal of heat radiating from the metal of the capsule and he was careful not to touch it as he crawled to the hatchway and risked a look inside. He saw a tunnel about eight feet long that ended in a chamber where an eerie green light was glowing. He couldn't see all of the chamber but there were two Martians in the part he could see and another lying on the deck moving weakly, probably another casualty of the dynamite bombs. Moving as quietly as possible, he rested his rifle on the coping of the hatch and aimed it down the tunnel.

He could now see what the two unhurt Martians were up to. They were dragging a large black box toward the tunnel. Connected to the black box was a flexible cable and on the end of that was another of the heat-ray devices.

Just as Dylan leveled the rifle and took aim, the Martian nearest him swung its huge eyes in his direction. The creature's V-shaped mouth, with its pointed upper lip, opened and a yelping sound issued from it while one tentacle snaked toward a pouch at its side and with incredible swiftness produced a small tube-like instrument.

Dylan didn't wait to learn what kind of hand weapon the Martians had. His rifle held a magazine with eight solid, hardened lead slugs. He squeezed the trigger eight times in rapid succession and had the satisfaction of seeing the tentacle with the weapon writhe and the tube fall to the deck. Three or four other slugs struck the oily gray body and the Martian jerked and flapped at itself before collapsing backward in a squirming heap. He wasn't sure whether he had killed the thing or not and he didn't have time to waste wondering. Jamming a second magazine into the rifle as the remaining Martian crawled toward the newly wounded one, Dylan caught a movement out of the corner of his eye and spotted another dark bulk coming into view holding another of the tubes.

Aiming for the eyes, Dylan snapped off a quick shot. The thing screamed and one large luminous orb disappeared in a splash of black blood. Then there was a a sudden flash and Dylan ducked. The one unwounded Martian had picked up its companion's weapon and fired it.

There was a hissing sound and a ball of fire streaked past Dylan's cheek, singeing it, and plowed into the mud with a sputtering sound. He ducked beneath the coping to get out of the way of the second fireball and was unable to get off a return shot. The yelpings from inside the capsule told him there was more than one survivor, and if they could keep him away from the hatch with hand weapons, they would have time to set up the heat-ray. He had to stop that at all costs, even if it meant exposing himself to empty his magazine into the capsule cabin.

Moving into what he thought would be the best position, he suddenly stood up with his head and shoulders over the coping, leveled the rifle and sent seven slugs down the tunnel. Then he threw himself flat again as perhaps ten fireballs went hissing overhead or ricocheted off the sides of the tunnel, spattering burning embers in all directions. His only reward for the desperate chance he had taken was a single keening yelp.

He could hear slithering sounds in the tunnel and knew the Martians must be coming up it, covering their progress with a hail of fire. Cursing, Dylan slammed another clip into the rifle and moved to one side, hoping to get in a few shots as they reached the opening. But he knew it was a futile effort. In the face of the fireballs, he couldn't keep the things penned in with rifle fire, and once out . . .

"Dylan, look behind you!" Clarinda's voice came to him. "Look what's comin' toward you, darlin' man!"

Dylan looked over his shoulder and saw three dynamite bombs floating through the air toward him in V-formation. As they came closer, they neatly and conveniently rearranged themselves into single file so he could grab them easily.

He captured the first one gratefully and then searched frantically in his pockets for a match. He had lost the lit cigar during his efforts at the capsule opening, and now he found he didn't have a match.

"Clarinda, throw me a box of matches! I haven't got a match to light the damn thing!"

The girl was standing on the rim of the crater, oblivious to her own safety, dress held up around her knees with one hand while she aimed a revolver with the other.

"Hold the bomb up and shut your eyes and I'll light it for you!" she shouted.

"Clarinda, don't!" Dylan yelled, but she had already pulled the trigger. Something fanned his face and the fuse sizzled into flame.

There wasn't time to wonder how she'd done it. The fuse was burning and the sounds of slithering were getting closer to the hatch. Waiting until the last possible second so there wouldn't be time to throw the bomb back at him, he tossed it down the tunnel and took off.

The explosion shook the capsule and Dylan's ears rang with the concussion. Clarinda sat down abruptly and stared down at him.

"Are you all right, darling?" he asked.

"Well, I've got two ears ringin' themselves off and a bottom that's achin' from sittin' down so sudden on a rock. I'm also half blinded by the flash, but I'm still alive, so I guess you could be sayin' I'm all right."

Thunder shook the ground again as another capsule streaked across the horizon to crash into a heavily wooded area a mile or so away.

"Damn! As fast as we destroy them, they keep coming in!" he said, scrambling back up the bank to join the girl.

Churchward was waving with his hat from the rim of the next crater. "We got this one! How about yours?"

"It's finished too!" Dylan shouted and got to his feet, slinging the rifle over his shoulder and turning to help Clarinda up. Suddenly he remembered the other two dynamite bombs that the girl had floated down to him and turned to look for them.

"Never mind them two," Clarinda said. "They're good little bombs and will follow along on their own till I tell them not to."

A sudden inspiration struck Dylan. "Clarinda, if you can transport those bombs through the air like that, you could levitate them into the capsules before they open up! That would be perfect! We could wipe them out as fast as we could make bombs."

She shook her head emphatically. "No! I could send a bomb through the invisible, aye, but do to it me mind would have to go along and . . ." She paused, looking startled, and swung around toward where several more craters were visible. "There's four of them over there, Dylan, and they're all opening at the same time. Somehow them beasties know what's happenin' outside and have changed the timing for their hatch openings so they coincide."

"That's all we need!" Dylan groaned.

"Three more over that way," she said, pointing. "Even the ones that are still too hot are taking a chance so they can get the heat-rays into action, I guess."

"Where next, Miss Clarinda?" Churchward shouted as the three men and Lady Philippa hurried toward them.

"Everywhere," Clarinda said, sweeping her arm around the horizon. "The Martians are all openin' their capsules at the same time."

"We'll have to split up," H. said crisply. "One man to a capsule so we can get four of them at once, if we're lucky."

"Why not four men and two women?" Lady Philippa said. "That way we can get six. I'm able and willing. I helped bring this horror to Annwn, so why shouldn't I die fighting it?"

Clarinda sighed. "That's all very well for you, but my business is lovin', not killin'. I couldn't throw a bomb even at them filthy creatures."

"You can do something better," Dylan said. "You stay here in the shelter of this crater with all the bombs we have left and float them to us whenever we're ready for them."

The redhead nodded and sat down. "Yes, I can do that, and I can compose a prayer or two to Keridwen, 'cause even if you get five, there'll still be more spittin' fire at us."

She had barely finished speaking when another capsule thundered overhead and they watched with stricken faces as it impacted almost two miles away.

"We can't get them all," Dylan said, brushing his lips across Clarinda's and starting at a run toward one of the furthest sites so that the nearest one was left to Philippa and the ones in between to the three Earthmen. "We can't get them all, but we've got to try!"

A few minutes later he was on the rim of a crater where a capsule lay embedded in the mud with its hatch screwing off rapidly. He thought about staying where he was and lobbing a bomb into the opening as soon as it was fully opened but decided against it, since three out of four they had thrown previously had missed or fallen short of the mark. There had to be a better way. He looked at the metal craft still hot from its passage through the atmosphere and wondered how long it would take to burn through his boots. What he needed was some kind of protective covering, perhaps wet leaves wrapped around his feet, or—why not mud? He was standing in what he needed!

Hastily scooping up handfuls of the thick black mud, he plastered it on the soles, sides and tops of his boots, hoping the thick layer would keep his feet from being roasted while he balanced himself on the capsule ready to drop a dynamite bomb down the tunnel as the hatch fell away.

It wasn't easy scrambling up the sloping hull of the spaceship, which was lying at a forty-five degree angle. The mud hissed with every step and his balance was precarious, but he knew he didn't dare touch the capsule with his hands or the skin would be blistered off. Before he was halfway up to the nose, his feet were starting to get hot. In a few minutes, it would be unbearable.

Clarinda, darling, send me a bomb, he whispered with his mind, *and you'd better light it because the hatch cover is about to go.*

You want me to shoot it alight or send a fire elemental to torch it off? she asked, humor bubbling to the surface even in the midst of terror.

Just strike a match in the air, if you please.

The bomb came hurrying toward him just as another Martian ship came hurtling out of the heavens and landed among tall trees to the north of the original landing site. The Martians were adjusting the trajectory to land further away so they couldn't be attacked as easily.

Fighting back a wave of despair, Dylan gripped the lighted bomb, leaned forward as the hatch fell away and pitched the missle down the tunnel into the bowels of the Martian craft. Then he leaped outward and landed in the soft mud, wincing at the ear-shattering blast that was followed by several other secondary explosions.

He didn't need to look to know his bomb had done its job. Nothing could possibly have survived in the close confines of the cabin with that bomb exploding in their midst. There was no need and no time to examine the craft more closely. He had to get on to the next one. He scrambled up the side of the crater, breathing heavily and beginning to feel exhaustion creeping up on him.

Dylan! Dylan, me love! Philippa and Dr. W. missed their targets and the Martians are out! Clarinda screamed in his mind. *They're settin' up the heat-rays in the craters and gettin' ready to lift them out!*

Which craters? Maybe there's still time if I can—

"Captain MacBride, is that you?" a familiar voice called from close by. "It's Asbury, skipper. I've come with the sappers and other volunteers."

The first officer of the *Thunderbolt* was running toward Dylan with the ex-servicemen hurrying after him carrying satchel charges and other mine-laying equipment.

"Hurry, it's almost too late!" Dylan shouted. "The Martians are setting up heat-rays in two of the craters. We've got to destroy them quick or it's—"

It was already too late. The camera-like apparatus appeared over the rim of the next nearest crater and began to swing into position.

"Into this crater quick!" Dylan yelled at the approaching men. "Run for your lives!"

The black box was swiveling in their direction and starting to smoke and hiss. Dylan emptied his rifle at it, hoping to hit the eye-like opening, while the first group of ex-servicemen came tumbling over the rim of the pit and slid down inside it.

The shots had no effect and the heat-ray licked out. Dylan shoved two men who were hesitating so they fell and rolled down the slope as he threw himself flat beside them. There was a scream behind them and a man crumpled on the edge of the crater. Another slid down into it, smouldering and dead.

Asbury and the seven remaining men lay staring at their dead comrades in horror. The ray was hissing again and Dylan cursed, knowing it had located another target. A tremendous explosion followed almost immediately and rubble rained down on the huddled group.

"They must have set off some dynamite," Dylan said.

"The bos'n, Summers, and three other men were behind us with more satchel bombs," Asbury said, voice slurred with fear. "Wh-what do we do now, Captain?"

"We're pinned down. If we make a move, they'll incinerate us," Dylan said, "but if we just stay here, they'll get one of their battle machines built and be able to look down on us and incinerate us anyway."

That's if they don't use the black smoke to kill us like trapped rats, Clarinda said in his head. *Mr. H. is in a tree where he can see into one of the pits and they're up to something different than settin' up the heat-ray. He's going to try to get a few shots at them with his rifle.*

Dylan explained the situation to the men crouched about him, concluding, "They'll burn him out of the tree if they see him. I wish we could create some kind of diversion."

"Why don't we rush 'em, sir?" one of the ex-soldiers suggested, fixing his bayonet and looking as though he'd relish a charge across the hundreds of yards of open salt marsh that lay between them and the crater where the Martians were working to set up a battle machine.

Dylan tried to think what would be best to do. If they all died here and now, there would be no one to carry the warning back to Avallon. Lombosa and his crew aboard the *Thunderbolt* were almost totally ignorant of what was going on. It would be hard enough to convince the authorities of what was coming if everyone here survived to spread the word. Without them, the city might be caught completely by surprise when the great striding battle machines of the invaders appeared outlined against the sky, lashing out with heat-rays and throwing the strangling smoke.

Since their mission to stop the Martian landing had failed, the only reasonable thing to do was retreat in the hope of fighting another day.

Is there any way you and Philippa can get away? Dylan asked Clarinda.

There's one of them things about three hundred yards from us. I can see their devil ray restin' on the side of the pit, she said. *They'd burn us to cinders if we tried to leave here.*

But you could get away without them seeing you, Dylan said, remembering how she had teleported them out of Cythraul's disintegrating caverns. *You could send yourself all the way to Avallon and probably take Philippa with you.*

And what would be happenin' to you, me bucko, and the others, while I was flyin' through the air draggin' that blackheaded hussy along with me?

We'll stay here and harass the Martians any way we can.

Harass them, eh? Harass them by supplying them with targets for their devil gun," Clarinda said. *No, I'm not goin' and leavin' you, and that's final!*

Then can you get us all out of here?

No. There's a limit to the power. It's like you can't overload one of them airships. You can't overload the power either. You can only throw yourself so far and only carry so much with you.

Several quick shots rang out from the fringe of high trees that surrounded the salt marshes to the north. The shots were followed by an explosion in one of the craters and then flame and black oily smoke shot upward from the pit.

Mr. H. got a couple of the monsters and blew up one of their smoke mortars, Clarinda reported from her psychic observation post. *He says to stay clear of that smoke driftin' off to the west.*

The hissing of one and then a second heat-ray filled the air, and risking a quick look, Dylan saw beams leaping from two craters toward the line of trees where H. and his friends were hiding.

"Damn them! We've got to do something! They'll burn the whole forest down to get at them."

"How about we rush them while they're busy?" suggested the man with his bayonet fixed, testing the blade with his thumb.

"If we spread out and went in fast, most of us might make it, skipper," Asbury urged.

Dylan knew they didn't really understand the problem. If they left the shelter of this crater and tried to dash across to the one occupied by the Martians, they would be cut down in seconds by a swathlike sweep of the heat-ray. Even if they succeeded in reaching the first pit, they'd come under fire from the others further on and be no better off than they were now.

Still, he had to do something. The Martians were systematically torching the forests to the north. Even if the three Earthmen had managed to escape the first blasts, they would sooner or later be incinerated by the beams of death that were devastating the trees. He couldn't just lie here and watch his friends be killed. He had to do something even if he knew it was hopeless.

"All right, let's go," he said to the men. "We'll rush them. And I guess you might as well fix bayonets and we'll do it in style."

Dylan, don't be an idiot! Clarinda screamed in his mind. *Don't do it! You don't have a chance!*

We don't have a chance anyway. As soon as we're finished, you and Philippa get out of here fast!

No, no, Keridwen, don't let him, don't—

But Dylan was already scrambling out of the crater with the eight men behind him. Each had a rifle and a haversack of dynamite bombs. They were trained fighting men so they spread out into a skirmish line without being told. Bending low, they sprinted toward the closest Martian-held mound.

It may have been that the Martians' attention was concentrated on the woods or perhaps it was just the audacity of a handful of men daring to charge them that stayed the aliens' hands long enough for the forlorn charge to cover half the distance to the target crater. Then they acted. Conscious that his breath was coming in shallow gasps and that fear was gripping his guts, Dylan saw the camera-like death machine rise above the lip of the round hole in the mud and begin to smoke. He dropped to one knee and blasted away at it with his rifle in a desperate attempt to knock it out before it engulfed them in flame.

His shots had no effect and the deadly beam of energy lashed through the air toward them. Asbury, several feet to Dylan's left and slightly ahead of him, became a torch. The man to Asbury's left screamed once and fell dying.

Astonished to find himself still alive, Dylan dashed forward, lighting a dynamite bomb as he went. When he was just a few feet from the crater, there was a roar in the sky above him. He thought at first it was another Martian spaceship but then a shadow passed across the ground—a huge, cigar-shaped shadow.

The heat-ray stopped pivoting as the Martians were also distracted by the sound of gasoline engines and the sight of two airships speeding toward their positions.

"It's the *Vengeance* and *Flying Cloud!* Dylan shouted. "They must have seen the capsules landing and come at full speed. Take cover, men, help is here!"

Dylan and the four men who had survived the mad charge dashed back to the protection of their crater as the *Vengeance* with Gatling guns blazing swept down on one Martian pit and the *Flying Cloud* on another. Despite their super-weapons, the Martians were momentarily at a disadvantage. Their battle machines were not yet ready and the rays took time to maneuver and aim. As they tried to readjust the angle of focus, first one and then the other crater was raked by steel-jacketed slugs from guns that could fire thousands of rounds a minute.

The devastating gun fire was followed by dynamite bombs falling from the airships as they passed overhead. Two Martian capsules and their full crews were wiped out in the first assault from the air.

Dylan, now's the time to get out, Clarinda said. *We'll*

never get another chance.

She was right. The Martians were fully occupied with the aerial attack. If they were ever going to escape and spread the alarm, it must be now. Dylan turned to his men. "Let's go! We have to get back to the *Thunderbolt!*"

Clarinda and Philippa were waiting at the edge of the thick foliage that encircled the camp. The redhead threw herself on Dylan.

"Oh, love, you're all right! You've not even got a singed hair! Praise Keridwen's sacred bosom!"

Dylan embraced her briefly, then grabbed each woman by the hand and hurried them down the trail with the four mercenaries at their heels. He risked one last look over his shoulder as he heard the familiar express train roar of a Martian rocket hurtling down. The *Vengeance* and *Flying Cloud* were still circling the landing site, firing their guns and dropping bombs, but now the heat-rays were starting to lick skyward.

"Get out, Noel, get out!" Dylan said, wishing he could shout in his friend's mind like Clarinda did in his. "Get out before they torch you off!"

He winced as the *Vengeance* climbed sharply to escape a lancing beam of heat, and he groaned as the *Flying Cloud* was hit aft by a beam that burned away half of her cabin but luckily missed the gas bag above it. Then he breathed a sigh of relief as he saw the two airships drift away toward the east, still firing their Gatlings as they retreated.

"Thank God," he said to the girls. "Churchward and the others may be dead but at least Noel and van Rasselway got away."

"Thank Keridwen, all three Earthmen are still alive too," Clarinda told him. "They were hidin' in a gully with their heads under water when the devil ray struck the first time and they ran for it before the forest was set afire. They're circling around the other way to join us at the ram."

"Then let's hurry!" Dylan urged. "We must get back to Avallon and spread the alarm."

"If anyone will listen," Clarinda said.

"They'll have to listen to me," Philippa said.

"Aye, and to Noel and van Rasselway and their crews," Dylan said. "This time they'll have to believe!"

Chapter 15

Every church bell and factory whistle in the city of
Avallon and its environs sounded out in wild alarm when the
first Martians were seen looming over the low hills across
the Silver Strand. Three battle machines on their spidery legs
were spotted from church towers and the crow's nests of
ironclads in the estuary on the tenth morning after the
Thunderbolt had hurried down the Myrk River with the
fearful news.

Pursued by several battle machines, the *Thunderbolt* had
been forced to submerge by day and travel on the surface
only at night, but had reached St. Rory in time to rouse the
garrison. The flying batteries and Border Horse Mountain In-
fantry had valiantly attempted to halt the advance of the
Martians on the frontier post. They were brushed aside with
the infernal death rays and gas. The old gunboat *Helios* took
out one Martian with gunfire as the aliens forded the Myrk
two miles above St. Rory, but the ship was destroyed a few
moments later by the concentrated fire of half a dozen heat-
rays. The Martians moved on toward the town.

The river port was already being evacuated, panicky
residents pouring across the Medelgo River bridges or heading downriver aboard steamers and lesser craft. As the first
Martians entered the town from the west and the remnants
of the defense forces fell back across the bridges, sappers of
the Empress's Own Border Rangers blew up the bridges
behind them, trapping several thousand refugees on the
western side of the river.

Those who failed to get across the bridges or away in
river craft tried to escape into the woods to the south, only
to perish when the aliens set the timber on fire.

The Martians seemed intent on wiping out the last vestiges
of human life in the St. Rory area, moving along the river
firing canisters of poisonous smoke at the masses of refugees

on the far side. A westerly wind blew the smoke across the battery of light artillery positioned at the narrows below the town to resist a crossing. Most of the gun crews died along with the fleeing refugees.

By the time of the disaster at St. Rory and the Medelgo bridges, the *Thunderbolt* was already at Camlam taking on coal for the dash up Lake Regillos to Avallon. Dylan went immediately to the telegraph office and wired General Horwitz that the invasion had begun and they had failed to crush it. *Urge city be placed in state of defense and naval forces prepare to dispute the crossing of Silver Strand. Urge partial evacuation of civilian population,* the message ended.

It was at the telegraph office that Dylan learned of the slaughter at St. Rory and of a second menace. The line from Ogmore in the Prefecture of the West had ceased to function after reporting that strange steel giants had been seen walking out of Westwind Pass.

"They're moving directly on Byras and Imola," Dylan told Churchward and the others. "That's the direct route to Avallon."

"My late friends made sure the Martians had good intelligence reports," Lady Philippa said sadly.

"They'll be at Avallon in a week at that rate," Dylan said.

"Keridwen save us all!" Clarinda said, biting her full lower lip with even white teeth. "Those heathen in the Ambrosial City and me little ones still in Trogtown! Himself will never forgive me if anything happens to the darlin's."

"Don't worry, we'll get there first," Dylan said and went to give orders to the *Thunderbolt* under way.

They reached Avallon a few days before the Martians reached Byras. They found the city astir although it was barely dawn when they pulled alongside their berth in the Old South Docks. The streets were alive with people. Hansoms, steam wagons and electrocars were delivering fashionably dressed citizens to the big white lake steamers. There was an air almost of an excursion cruise on the ships, with bands playing and people waving, but most of those going aboard were carrying suitcases and lorries loaded with luggage were lined up near the ships' cargo hatches.

"The fancy are gettin' their precious hides out first as usual," Clarinda said, "but this time, I can't say I blame them."

From where Dylan and Clarinda stood on the conning tower of the ram, they could see the Cyved and Amion roads that ran through the lowlands south of the city. Both were jammed with a slow-moving double line of people and vehicles.

There was also other activity in the city. As their hansom drove along the embankment near Greenfields, they saw pioneers of the Third and Fifth Fusiliers digging rifle pits. Further on they passed patrols of Light Dragoons and Yeomanry brilliant in scarlet, yellow and vermilion uniforms, some accompanied by their packs of hounds as became mobilized hunt clubs.

"Surely you do not intend to use those buffoons in cavalry charges against the Martian heat-rays," Mr. H. said to the young staff officer from Horwitz's staff who met them.

"The Dux Bellum called them up to help in crowd control," the adjutant said dryly. "Now we'll probably have to detail some Border Horse to control them."

"It's guns that are going to be needed," Dylan said. "Guns of every description, the bigger the better."

"The guns of the old forts to the north of the city and along the Strand are being reconditioned as quickly as possible," the officer said. "Every railway to north and east is crowded with trains bringing artillery from seize guns to pom-poms."

"What about warships?" Dylan asked. "A concentration of ironclads in the Strand might be able to prevent the Martian crossing."

"The Ice Sea fleet has been ordered to come south," the man said, "and the Lake Squadron is moving into position."

"Good! We'll add the *Thunderbolt* to their number. I have a reserve commission. I'll go to the Admiralty at once and ask for command of the ram."

"Dylan, no, you've done enough," Clarinda objected. "We can go to Hibernia or even your dreadful wilderness in Vineland. Let's take the wee ones and get out now. Himself, me father, has a fine great house in County Fagin where we could live. He'd have the children there with him except that he's never home, always followin' his profession to all parts of the world. He'd be happy for us to have the house."

"And how long do you think it would be before the Martians come to Hibernia?" Dylan asked.

"Oh, but they wouldn't dare! The gods would strike them dead!"

"Avallon is the Ambrosial City, sacred to more gods then all the counties of Hibernia."

"Then they wouldn't dare when they found out how me people can fight," the girl said. "They're demons when they're aroused."

"Then get yourself aroused," Dylan said. "Help us with your powers to stop the Martians."

"I can't . . . I never could . . . not what you mean," she wailed, turning pale and beginning to shake. "It's too horrible . . . too horrible!"

She pressed her face into his shoulder, sobbing, and Dylan wondered again at the depth of her terror. There could be no doubt that it was very real, and he was beginning to think it had some connection with the power; perhaps it was a basic cosmic fear, handed down to her by the so-called Elder Race, some remembrance from the misty beginnings of time when the gods had battled the giant kraken for survival.

Clarinda raised her tear-stained face. "Will you go with me and the kiddies, love?"

"No," he said, kissing her trembling lips. "It's my duty to remain here, but you must go and take the children. I'll arrange for your transportation and—"

"Forget it. I'll stay in me temple and hold Keridwen's hand till the end," she said. "I'll not run away and leave you to get your fool self killed."

Dylan reported to the Admiralty and received command of the *Thunderbolt* and a navy crew to man her. In a time of universal terror, the military bureaucracy could stir itself into action, and terror there certainly was.

General Sir Abercrombie Fitz-Hugh and the Third Field Army had tried to defend the approaches of Byras and Imola against the Martian advance. Fifteen thousand troops with a hundred big guns and the support of three armed airships had fought a three-day battle against approximately fifty Martians; the result had been a worse disaster than the Battle of Killiwic during the Goggish War. The masked batteries and hurriedly placed mine fields of the Avallonian forces had destroyed five and damaged another five Martian battle machines, but ten thousand troops had died from the enemy heat-rays and choking smoke. Every gun had been lost and two of the three airships demolished, one by a Martian flying machine armed with a heat-ray.

The remnants of Fitz-Hugh's army and a few thousand refugees from the two cities reached Ragnor in the Imola Hills the night before the first Martians loomed over those same low hills and were visible from Avallon itself.

Now Dylan stood on the bridge of the *Thunderbolt* and watched with binoculars a battery of howitzers in Fort Coily shelling five Martian battle machines. On every side of the ram were dozens of steamers and sailing craft loaded with frightened people fleeing from Avallon, Ragnor and Coily, heading north up the Silver Strand.

As the first bursts of shellfire appeared near the first Martian, the thing swung around and moved rapidly down the embankment on which the railroad between Imola and Ragnor was built. It seemed to be trying to get closer to the gun emplacements. Perhaps, Dylan thought, the heat-ray was outranged by the ancient guns of the fort.

One shell landed almost at the feet of the leading Martian and one spiderlike leg seemed to buckle. The Martian crashed forward and lay struggling to rise on the railroad right-of-way. Another shell fell within a few feet of the thing and a cheer went up from the ships scurrying before the oncoming menace.

"Good shooting!" Dylan said, slapping the young lieutenant who was his executive officer on the back. "First blood to the army."

Two more Martians were advancing cautiously down the track as though feeling their way through the mines that had been laid by sappers from every regiment in the city during the last few days.

The battle machines were now about half a mile from the bank of the Silver Strand and were still under fire from the fort and a battleship whose top works could be dimly seen beyond the massed fleet. Behind the alien pair, obviously scouts, Dylan could see at least a dozen more of the things heading toward the estuary.

"Those first two are in the mine fields now, sir," Lieutenant Fenshaw said.

"Yes, and I hope to God the commander of the sappers has his head about him and holds off until the others move up," Dylan said.

"Those two almost seem to be looking for the mines,"

Fenshaw said. "Do you suppose they have some way of detecting them?"

"They've probably seen some of their companions hit by mines and are just being careful," Dylan said. "I hope the sapper commander is just as careful. That system of mines could destroy most of those in sight if he waits and—"

A thunderous blast interrupted him and the whole area where the two Martians were seemed to lift skyward as nearly two hundred mines went off in rapid succession.

The *Thunderbolt* and the ships around it rocked wildly from the concussion, and Dylan could see nothing of the two Martian scouts through the dissipating smoke and falling debris. But off in the distance, untouched by the blast, were twelve Martians and at least twenty more behind them, all moving steadily toward the city.

"I guess the sappers touched off the mines prematurely," Fenshaw said sadly.

"Or perhaps the Martians did it themselves, sacrificing two of their number to the greater good," Dylan said. "Beyond doubt they are capable of it."

"What do we do now?"

"Now it's up to us," Dylan told him. "Get up steam, Mr. Fenshaw. We're standing down channel to protect the shipping."

The hundreds of diverse ships were in real danger and so were the thousands of refugees who jammed their decks. If the Martians, no longer troubled by the mine fields and advancing in tremendous distance-eating strides, were to get among these craft, the slaughter would be terrible indeed.

"Sound our siren and air horn!" Dylan shouted as the first Martian reached the shore and started wading out toward the northward-fleeing armada. "Full steam up, mister! We're going through the fleet at full speed!"

Three small armored gunboats were all that lay between the refugee fleet and the six Martians who were now wading out toward it. The howitzers at the forts to the south and the long rifles of one fort to the north were pouring a heavy fire into the main body of Martians moving through the area ploughed up by the exploding mines, but the guns couldn't bring the six leading battle machines under fire because of the danger of hitting the fleeing ships.

"Come right sharply, helmsman," Dylan ordered as the *Thunderbolt* began her dash through the panicked merchant ships weaving back and forth, blowing their whistles and giving off great volumes of smoke. "Come right sharply and steady on the water tower at the Imola Hills. I want to pass between that Nordlands Line steamer and the tug astern of her."

"Aye, aye, sir," the helmsman said, eyeing the wildly maneuvering ships apprehensively.

"If we catch any of the blighters on our ram, they've had it," Fenshaw said, hanging onto the binnacle as the *Thunderbolt* heeled over in the wake of a big liner and righted herself with a shudder.

"So have we," Dylan said, "but the only thing we're going to catch on our ram is a few Martians, if we're lucky."

"The forts to the south of the city have come under air attack, sir," reported the lookout in the ram's abbreviated top hamper.

Taking his eyes off the writhing ships for a moment, Dylan saw two round-bodied flying machines circling lazily above the fort. As he watched, one of the disks swooped in low and left a heavy pall of thick oily smoke behind it. Dylan cursed, sick at heart, as he saw the smoke settle like the hand of death over the fort and heard one gun after another grow silent. Then his attention was yanked back to the *Thunderbolt's* mad dash through the fleet.

She had passed between a large paddle-wheeled steamer, from whose decks a spontaneous chorus of cheers greeted her, and a chugging little tramp that had refugees clinging even to the superstructure.

"Come left smartly!" Dylan yelled as out of the drifting, smoky haze there suddenly emerged a big white yacht with the Imperial crest on her bow and white foam boiling behind her.

The *Thunderbolt* heeled over and turned quickly, her deadly ram showing briefly through the white wake of the fleeing yacht.

"Well, we almost got a member of the Imperial family that time," Dylan said.

"Are they really fleeing, sir?" Fenshaw asked, seeming to find the thought of a descendant of Arthur Pendragon's fleeing battle more horrifying than the prospect of their imminent life and death struggle with six Martians.

There was no time for Dylan to answer because looming directly ahead of them was the long low silhouette of a loaded ore carrier, decks crowded with refugees as well as piles of coal.

"Sound three short blasts on the air horn!" Dylan shouted. "All astern full! Right hard rudder!"

The boiling ram of the *Thunderbolt* scraped paint off the stern quarter of the carrier as the ironclad swung desperately and backed down to avoid the merchant ship and then pushed clear of the main body of the refugee fleet.

The sight that greeted them once they were clear of the fleet was terrifying. Half a dozen ships were burning from the effects of the Martian heat-rays. People could be seen throwing themselves overboard and scores of heads were already bobbing about in the water. One of the three armored gunboats was ablaze from stem to stern; another lay dead in the water, wisps of the strangling smoke drifting around her. The third gunboat and an armed merchant cruiser were still firing at the advancing Martians with four- and five-inch guns but the effect seemed to be negligible, since only one battle machine had been downed.

"Flag hoist on *Furious*, Captain," reported the chief signalman, who had his glass trained on the flagship of the ironclads. "Our pennant. It reads, 'Engage the enemy off your bow.'"

"Thanks," Dylan said. "That's pretty much what we had in mind."

"Is that a reply, sir?"

"No. Just hoist 'Affirmative.'"

"Aye, aye, sir."

Dylan watched with growing apprehension as the five remaining Martians, supported now by seven more on shore, waded further out into the estuary until their tripod legs were almost totally submerged and water was lapping around the cupolas which held the aliens and their weapons. This way they appeared much less formidable and also presented a far better target for the ram of the *Thunderbolt* if she could get in range.

Suddenly a heat-ray lashed out from the battle machine furthest to the north, its target a large passenger ship which had been in a collision with another craft and was limping along with her bow heavily damaged. The *Thunderbolt's* captain and crew watched helplessly as death flickered along the crowded decks, sickened by the ghastly carnage and appalled by the ease with which the ray holed the ship twice, leaving her aflame and sinking fast.

Seconds later the last remaining gunboat blew up and the armed merchant ship drifted away in a cloud of black smoke, her guns silenced forever.

"All hands below!" Dylan ordered. There was only one way the *Thunderbolt* could get close enough to the Martians to use her ram, and that was to submerge. "All hands below! Dog down all watertight doors, blow air from tanks and start taking on ballast!"

Taking the helm while the quartermaster hurried to the other wheel in the pilothouse, Dylan saw the nearest Martian aim its gas-launching weapon at the ram. Just at the moment he saw it let fly with a black cylinder, he felt the tug of the quartermaster's hands on the helm. He let go the wheel to dive through the only remaining open hatch as the *Thunderbolt* put her bow down and water started closing over her as she submerged. An instant before the hatch was slammed shut behind him and watertight integrity established throughout the ship, he saw the gas canister splash against the rounded side of the ironclad, bounce back and explode into thick, oily black death.

Fortunately, the *Thunderbolt* was airtight as well as watertight, and as the black smoke swirled about her, Dylan suddenly realized that it screened their movements more effectively than even a deliberately laid smoke screen would have done. Although he couldn't see the Martians through the periscope or the narrow glass-covered eye slits in the tip of the conning tower that remained above water, they couldn't see the ram either and that was a great advantage at the moment.

Heat-rays lashed through the smoke twice but they were aiming for a ship floating on the surface, not one almost completely submerged. All that happened to the *Thunderbolt* as she edged through the thick oiliness was that her flying bridge, where Dylan had been standing just a few moments ago, dissolved as the ray struck it.

"Stand by to ram, all hands!" Dylan ordered.

Bringing the ship around on a parallel course, Dylan steered due south for ten minutes. Now when the partially submerged ship came out of the smoke with only the round top of her conning tower and periscope showing, the Martians would be far less likely to spot her at once.

"It's getting thinner now," Fenshaw said, peering through

the periscope while Dylan used the glass-covered slit. "We'll be out of it in a minute or two."

"All ahead full!" Dylan ordered as the ship broke out into the bright sunlight. He swung her due west again and saw the round cupola of a Martian dead ahead at less than five ship's lengths.

"Stand by, all!" Dylan ordered.

The Martian, realizing that something was happening on its blind side, swung the little turret on top of the cupola which held the ray-gun and smoke mortar. Dylan saw the camera device swivel toward them and leaned forward as though pushing the ship faster. Now it was a race between the heat-ray and the boiling ram of *Thunderbolt*'s bow. For a few breathless seconds it was hard to tell who would win. The heat-ray had started to smoke; there was the whining hiss of its warming up as the first thin beam raised steam about twenty feet off their port bow. But the ram had won—she had sheared off one leg of the Martian's tripod. The thing was collapsing, to be hit by the steel point and sliced open. Dylan caught a brief glimpse of the superstructure of the battle machine falling on the deck of the *Thunderbolt* and being swept aside to sink in her wake.

"Dive . . . dive . . . dive!" Dylan yelled and hit the diving alarm on the bulkhead beside him.

The *Thunderbolt* shuddered and sank to periscope level again as the massed heat-rays of the four remaining Martians slashed at her. Dylan had already picked out his next target, a battle machine about a dozen cable lengths toward the shore. He had gotten a quick bearing on it and was holding to a course that would take him under it.

"Target bearing zero three zero," Fenshaw said, eyes glued to the periscope. "It's whirling its turret and blazing away in all directions with that heat-ray. It's stirring up a steam bath that will make it twice as hard to see our periscope."

"It won't know we're on it until we come up right underneath," Dylan said. "Then it'll be too late. Stand by to retract periscope on order."

Even in the airtight submerged ram they could hear the whine of the Martian's ray device as it fired blindly into the rising steam.

"It's getting hot in here," someone remarked.

"It's hotter out there in the water," another seaman said.

"Two cable lengths now," Fenshaw said, his voice a kind of hoarse whisper as though he thought the Martian might hear him if he spoke too loudly.

"One cable length," Fenshaw said, and Dylan gripped the helm tightly and held on. "Half a cable length."

"Now! On it . . . under it."

The ram shuddered and shook as they smashed through the legs of the second Martian like papier-mâché, then partially surfaced, smashing the cupola of the falling alien with the turtle back.

Debris crashed against the conning tower and was shrugged away aft. Through the eye slit, Dylan saw the round rubbery torso of the Martian, covered with black blood from a dozen wounds, trying to cling to a stanchion on the port side of the ship, but as the *Thunderbolt* nosed down again it was swept away to die in the ram's propellers.

"Two! We got two!" Fenshaw broke into a cheer and the rest of the crew took it up.

"Let's make it three," Dylan said, surfacing with the use of the diving fins to get his bearings. That was almost a fatal mistake because the heat-rays of the three remaining Martians converged on a spot only a ship's length aft of the ironclad.

In the few seconds they had been on the surface, Dylan had made out the position of another Martian. He had also seen a towering splash of water near it that must have been made by a shell from at least a ten-inch gun. He breathed a quick little prayer that the Avallonian battleships shelling the Martians didn't put a salvo into the *Thunderbolt* instead.

"They're running for it," Fenshaw reported as he saw the Martians start to withdraw toward shallower water. "We've got them on the run!"

Dylan brought the ram around in a wide circle to catch the aliens by surprise, by approaching submerged from another direction and cutting off the nearest battle machine from the shallow water. He guessed they weren't so much running from their single adversary as they were trying to draw the *Thunderbolt* into an area where the ram couldn't dive.

"Don't let them get away!" Fenshaw was yelling. "Sink them all!"

The Martians were turning the waters of the Silver Strand into a boiling cauldron and the heat inside the ship was approaching the unbearable as she drove through clouds of steam toward the battle machine whose escape route they had managed to intersect.

The Martian didn't see the ram until the ship was almost on it and then it was too late and the ship too close for the heat-ray. All the Martian could do was try to sidestep the steel beak of the ship. It almost succeeded, taking huge strides although hampered by the depth of the water. Almost wasn't good enough. The *Thunderbolt's* ram sheared off two legs and the Martian tumbled into the water, its mechanical voice hooting wildly. As the cupola bobbed in the water off to starboard, Dylan saw its hatch open and tentacles appear as the occupant tried to climb out. Then water washed over it and it was gone. He watched for a swimming octopuslike creature to come into view but saw something else—a long torpedo shape and a fin.

It was a shark, probably drawn by the bleeding bodies in the water and the swimming survivors of the refugee ships. Two tentacles writhed above the surface of the water briefly and then disappeared, leaving a trail of black blood as the shark's fin sped on.

That quick flash of Earth monster and Martian monster in conflict brought back a vivid and horrifying memory to Dylan. He shivered involuntarily as the incident was something he preferred to keep repressed, but this time he welcomed it because it gave him an idea.

The *Thunderbolt* was turning back out into deeper water as salvos of shells began to fall all about her and the two remaining Martians. There was also heavy ray fire from the Martians along the shore, and the sea was boiling with the splash of heavy shell and heat from the rays.

"You're not going to let them get away, are you, Captain?" Fenshaw yelled. "Don't show them any pity! You know what they did in Byras and Imola!"

"And in St. Rory and right here," Dylan said, "but they're getting all they can handle right now. Look!"

A series of eleven-inch shells had straddled one of the Martians, and for a moment its fate was obscured by the sheets of water that were thrown up as well as by the steam that rose from it. Then, as the view cleared, Dylan could see the battle machine still toiling toward land, but only for a moment. The straddle was followed by a salvo and the Martian disappeared again in bursting shells and gigantic splashes of water. This time it didn't emerge.

"Let's get the last one!" Fenshaw shouted as he saw the Martian die.

"No, let's live to fight another day. If we—" Dylan's words were cut off by the terrible high-pitched hissing of a heat-ray and the *Thunderbolt* was shaken as though by a giant hand.

"We're hit aft!" someone yelled in the speaking tube. "We're holed and taking on water fast!"

Dylan swung the helm over sharply and headed the staggering ironclad toward the Avallon side of the Strand. She was already sluggish, but if he could get her into shallow water, they might be able to save her, or at least themselves.

The chief engineer's head appeared in the hatchway from below. "We're filling fast."

"Can you keep up steam?" Dylan asked.

"The boilers are guttering out now," the man said.

"We've still got way on," Dylan said. "Get your men topside. I'll try to ground her."

"I'll get what's left of them, sir. The ray and the boiling steam took their toll." The man left and when he returned he brought with him six other men, two of whom were being supported by their comrades.

"Stand by to abandon ship as soon as she grounds," Dylan said, thinking about the last time he had managed to put this craft ashore in the mudflats and how Clarinda had laughed and teased him until he had yanked her into the mud with him.

"She's settling fast," the chief said and went to join his weary men near the conning tower hatchway.

"Undog that hatch and prepare to open it," Dylan ordered, beginning to doubt that they were going to make it. It was almost a mile to shallow water, and if they went down in their present thirty fathoms . . .

There was very little way on now, and Dylan's hands were white-knuckled as he gripped the helm. "Stand by to abandon ship," he said.

The *Thunderbolt* shuddered and was dead in the water. "She's going!" somebody screamed, and the angle of the deck dropped sharply to aft.

"Abandon ship!" Dylan commanded, sounding the air horn continuously in hope of attracting the attention of rescue craft, although the possibility seemed slim in the middle of the disaster all around them.

The bos'n had put his shoulder to the deck-level hatch and tried to shove it open. It resisted him and water began seeping in.

"The hatch on top of the conning tower!" Fenshaw ordered. "Up the ladder quick!"

The men swarmed toward the ladder and up it just as the ship, which had been settling rapidly by the stern, suddenly jerked and heeled over to starboard.

"She's going! She's going!" several voices cried, and when the hatch was open, the men on the ladder scurried up it and out into the water.

"You next, sir," Fenshaw said, pushing Dylan toward the ladder.

"I'm the captain, I go last," Dylan said and almost lifted the slighter man onto the rungs of the ladder.

Fenshaw's feet disappeared out the hatch and Dylan was halfway up the ladder when the ram gave one last convulsive shudder and rolled over. Dylan hung there upside down in the total darkness with the water pouring in about him and thought ruefully that if he died now he'd never know what it would have been like to be married to Clarinda.

"No, no, no," Clarinda was saying to the four men who stood around the dais in her little temple with grim expressions on their faces.

"We saw it, Miss Clarinda," Churchward said. "We were in the Fusiliers' lookout station in the cathedral tower. We saw the whole thing through our glasses."

"A most extraordinary display of skill and courage it was, ma'am," Mr. H. said. "Dylan MacBride and his command single-handedly destroyed more Martians than the rest of the forces defending the city combined."

Clarinda said nothing. She seemed to be listening to the heavy cannonade that was still going on out in the estuary.

"Dylan died as he would have wanted to," Noel told her, "with the utmost courage."

"Yes," Dr. W. said. "I spoke to the few survivors from the *Thunderbolt* who managed to get ashore. Lieutenant Fenshaw, who was himself injured when the ram went down, said Dylan lifted him bodily onto the ladder to let him escape first. My dear, your fiancé died magnificently."

"No, no, no," Clarinda repeated. There were no tears in

her eyes and she seemed to be staring at something in the far distance.

"Now you must think of yourself, Clarinda," Noel said. "Yourself and the children. Lady Alice is leaving in the electrocar within the hour for our country estate in the Midlands. You're welcome to stay there as long as you wish or until your father comes for you."

"No. Himself is in Caer Arinhod, but I'm not leavin' here," she said in a steady, calm voice.

"But, Clarinda, the city is to be abandoned," Noel protested. "The ironclads have stopped the Martians briefly but their losses are staggering and General Horwitz has decided to withdraw the army. He plans to make a stand in the Northwind Mountains and along the shores of Lake Thryan and, if necessary, resort to guerrilla warfare. You see, you must leave."

"No, I won't," Clarinda said, shaking her head. "I can't leave. If I leave, Dylan will die."

The men looked at each other, obviously thinking that grief had unhinged the girl.

"But, my dear, he is already dead," Mr. H. said gently. "He went down with his ship."

"No, he's not dead . . . not yet," she said and touched her hand to her heart. "If he was dead, I'd be dead in here and I'm alive."

The men exchanged more glances, and Dr. W. tried to make her understand. "If you're thinking that he somehow managed to make it to shore, I must tell you that Fenshaw said he was still in the ship when she turned her bottom up and went down. He couldn't have escaped."

"He didn't escape," Clarinda said. "He went down with the ship and that's where he is—underwater but still alive."

Noel put out a sympathetic hand to the girl. "Clarinda, you've got to accept the truth."

"Poor lass, I'm afraid all this is too much for her sensitive nature," Dr. W. whispered to his friend.

"Perhaps you could give her a sedative," H. suggested.

"Under the water and alive," she repeated, "and I've got to figure some way to yank him out of thirty fathoms of water without drowning him, out of that iron sinking boat that I knew would be the death of him some day."

"Clarinda, you're talking nonsense," Noel said, placing a hand on her arm. "Your grief has—"

She shook off his hand and glared at him. "I'm not daft, mon! I have the sight. I *see* him. Even in the pitch dark I see him alive in the *Thunderbolt*. But he's in an air pocket that is fast disappearing and how am I going to get him out of there without givin' him the whatchamacallit—the bends?"

Chapter 16

Dylan stood on what had been the bottom rung of the ladder leading up to the flying bridge but which was now the top rung because of the *Thunderbolt*'s position. Hanging on with both hands as the water rose past his hips and then his waist, he wondered why he was bothering to make the effort to stay alive. Surely it would be better to get it over with fast than to stand here in the freezing darkness and wait for slow death to overtake him. There was no chance of rescue. The ship was down in at least thirty fathoms of water in the deep center of the estuary so no diving rig could possibly reach him even if, with the Martians at the gates, anyone knew what had happened to him or had the time to do anything about it.

It was a hell of a way to die for a man who had dreamed of opening up unknown parts of the world, who longed to explore the unseen and add knowledge to mankind's store. Anything would be better than drowning in an iron coffin in pitch darkness.

His service revolver was still strapped to his side and although it was wet it might still fire. Perhaps it would be better to get it over with.

He knew there was no way out. The hatch at the top of the conning tower was buried in the mud; the one on the side was held closed by water pressure; and even if he could force it open and shot to the surface, he would die slowly and horribly of the bends. And the water was rising.

"It's a great choice," he muttered to himself, "bubbles in my blood or water in my lungs. Maybe a bullet would be best after all." He reached for the revolver and pulled it part-way out, then let it drop back into the holster. It just wasn't in him to commit suicide.

The water was almost up to his shoulders now. He was standing with his head against what had been the deck of the conning tower so there was no place else to go.

"Poor Clarinda," he said out loud, just to keep himself company. "I wonder if she'll ever know what happened to me. I hope she goes back to Hibernia to stay with her father. Oh God, I hope the Martians never get to Hibernia!"

"Damn water is getting higher every minute. Guess I might as well keep talking because pretty soon I won't be able to."

The water was almost up to his chin and he was shivering from the cold and starting to gasp a little from the level of carbon monoxide that was building up. "Damn, I wish I could at least see. Dying in the dark is somehow worse than dying in the light."

The water was lapping at the point of his chin and he leaned his head back. "It won't be long now. I wonder what it's like to die. I guess I'll know in a few more minutes. Maybe I'll meet Keridwen in person." He giggled at his own babbling, knowing it was caused by the bad air and exhaus-tion, but beyond caring. "Wouldn't Clarinda be in a snit if I did? I could at least tell Keridwen that I came highly recommended by her one and only priestess. Oh, Keridwen, if only there was some light!"

And suddenly there was light. Not very much light, only a tiny spot of warm pink that glowed above his head.

"Now I'm starting to see things. I've got pink spots before my eyes. Lord, but I'm cold . . . cold enough to be dead already."

It was a ridiculous notion but the pink spot seemed to be growing and getting brighter and warmer. "I guess I must be dead already. Maybe the hereafter is a spot of warm pink light if you've lived a good life and a spot of dirty old cold brown if you've been a skunk."

The water was still rising but he was beginning to feel warmer as the pink spot grew larger. It was an hallucina-tion, of course, brought on by oxygen starvation, but what had appeared to be only a flat dot at first was taking on dimension and expanding into a ball of warm pinkness about a foot in diameter. The pink ball was getting so big, in fact, that there was hardly room for his head and it in the little remaining air space.

"I wonder if it could be static electricity, St. Elmo's fire?" he said, knowing very well it wasn't since he had seen St. Elmo's fire on the masthead of ships. "Well, at least it's keeping me warm. I'll not only die with my boots on but with my toes warm as well."

Then he felt the ball of pink pressing against his face. "Hey, what the devil!" he gasped and felt it closing about his head. Then he was staring out of the pink warmth at the water that had risen to the level of his nose. In some way he didn't understand, he was able to breathe in the bubble that had settled on his shoulders and enclosed his head.

"I can breathe . . . and talk in here," he said in surprise. "It's warm and the air smells good, kind of like perfume, subtle, exotic perfume that—Clarinda! I'm not hallucinating! Clarinda has sent me a bubble of air!"

There was no doubt in his mind now. Only the red-headed priestess smelled exactly the way the air in the bubble did. This was some of her magic and it had come just in time to keep him from drowning, but how long could it maintain him here in the depths of the sea? And how long could he stand being cooped up this way?

"Hey, the bubble is growing again! It's forcing the water out of the compartment! Don't tell me she's going to try to raise the *Thunderbolt!* No, she couldn't do that, it would strain her power."

Clarinda, darling, are you there? Can you hear me? There was no answer but the bubble continued to grow until his upper torso and then his lower torso were encased in warmth and comfort.

When he was completely inside the bubble, the water closed around it, rocking it gently and almost lulling him to sleep. He struggled to remain awake because he wanted to know what was going to happen next. Could she keep him alive indefinitely in this thing? Where was the oxygen coming from, he wondered, the warm, perfumed, obviously pressurized oxygen?

Clarinda, if you're just postponing the inevitable with this contraption, just giving me a few more hours of life trapped down here by myself, I'd rather—

Suddenly everything blacked out. He felt a tug at the

bubble, a tug at his mind and body and then nothing.

Dylan woke up on a pile of pillows in the rear alcove of Keridwen's temple. Bending over him was a freckle-faced girl of about eleven holding a fan in her hand. It was very hot in the alcove and sweat was standing out on his forehead.

"Are you Kathy?" he asked.

"I'm Dagda," the girl said sullenly.

"Where's your sister, Dagda?"

"Which sister?"

"Clarinda, of course."

"Clarinda, of course, is in bed. She's like to have died of mental fatigue and the vapors, thanks to you," the child said accusingly.

"Is she going to be all right?" Dylan asked, sitting up and checking to make sure he was all right himself. He could find no ill effects at all from his watery entombment.

"Of course you have none!" the girl said scornfully. "Me poor sister worked her mind to the bone to keep you pressurized for three days just like the Earth doctor said she should."

Dylan sighed. Dagda had read his mind but that shouldn't have surprised him. After all, she was Clarinda's sister and both her father and mother were said to have the power also.

"Dr. W. is here in the temple?"

"We're all here in the temple hiding from the Martians," the girl said. "That's why it's so hot. The Trogs have barricaded the gates 'cause the Martians burned and black-smoked half the city. They're up over our heads right now for all I know."

"I see. Well, would you ask Dr. W., Mr. H. and Major Churchward to come in here, please?"

"I will," the girl said ungraciously, "but I don't know why I take the trouble. I don't know why herself takes the trouble either. You're not all that grand without your kilts."

A few minutes later Mr. H. came into the alcove. He was wearing his deerstalker cap and two bandoliers of ammunition. There was a pouch of dynamite bombs at his hip and a rifle slung over his shoulder.

"Well, feeling a little more like yourself, are you?" he greeted Dylan. "W. is operating right now but he'll attend you shortly."

"I really don't need a Doctor," Dylan said. "I just wanted to know what's been happening. The child said I'd been out for three days."

"Your lady's doing," H. said. "She didn't want you fretting while you were being depressurized by her magical contraption so she kept you asleep."

"What about the city? Is the situation bad?"

"About as bad as bad can be," H. said gravely. "The fleet held the Martians for about six or seven hours, but the black smoke and the heat-rays finally got most of the ships and drove the rest off. Then the Martians waded—yes, waded—right across the Silver Strand, underwater, mind you, and were into the city before we knew they were coming. Luckily most of the population and General Horwitz' army had gotten out the night before with the government, but still there was horrible slaughter. God only knows how many died or how many more are trapped down here in Trogtown. Trapped and waiting for . . . well, for what?"

"I've got to get up," Dylan said. "I want to see Clarinda and then—"

"The poor thing is exhausted. Doctor gave her a sleeping powder and she'll probably sleep for another three or four hours."

"Poor Clarinda, and all for me," Dylan said.

"A gem of a woman, a perfect gem," H. said. "Intellectually, physically and what is more important for our purposes, psychically a gem. That contraption she created out of nothing was a wonder. I'd have dearly liked to study it but as soon as you didn't need it any more it vanished."

"What are our chances?" Dylan asked. "Is there any hope of winning against the Martians?"

H. shrugged his thin shoulders. "I'm not a man who despairs easily, MacBride, but I think there is none at all. Horwitz will fight on in the hills and other nations will resist, but in the end the heat-ray and the black smoke will conquer first Annwn and then Earth."

Dylan sighed. "Perhaps not Earth. There are the Guardians of the Gates, the cowled ones, and they are powerful too."

"Lady Philippa told me of a scheme worked out by her former friends in the Circle of Life to get around the Guardians," H. said. "Their fee, you know, for passage between the worlds is human life-force. The Martians already have thousands of human prisoners and will have millions more than they need for their feed lots and breeding pens. They can pay the Guardians any exorbitant fee they might ask for entry into Earth—pay it with human life."

Dylan got up and started looking for his clothes. He felt strong and rested, not like a man who had fought a dozen battles, traveled a thousand miles and been trapped in a steel coffin at the bottom of the sea. Clarinda's pink bubble deserved credit for that.

They found his kilt and other clothes piled on top of a hamper behind a flagon of cheap red wine that Clarinda kept for her devotees, and Dylan dressed quickly, buckling on his claymore and pistol last.

"You act like a man who has a plan," H. said.

"I have," Dylan said. "I'm going to commit suicide."

H. looked startled and shocked. "I suppose many will be coming to that conclusion in the next few weeks but I didn't expect you to be one of them."

"And I'm going to take as many Martians with me as I can."

"That sounds more promising," H. said. "We might all consider suicide under those conditions. How are you going to do it?"

"First tell me how many Martians there are. Are they all in the city proper or have they spread out?"

"There must be about fifty of them," H. said. "We haven't exactly been idle here in Trogtown, you know. I've been leading a valiant little band of redheaded scouts, age eight to fourteen—Clarinda's brothers. Smart little devils they are, too. Remind me of my old irregulars. We can get out of Trogtown through the sewers and other underground tunnels they know of, so we've kept a pretty close eye on the Martians these last few days."

"And what have you found?"

"As I said, there are about fifty of them still alive on Annwn, although I imagine that more will be coming eventually. They haven't pushed out of the city yet because they seem to be busy working on some new infernal machines, as though they needed more than they already have."

"Are they concentrated in any one place?" Dylan asked.

"Most of them are in the Greenfields area where your airships used to be hangared. They have set up a plant of some kind—amazing how those handling machines of theirs can build something overnight. They've set up a plant and are bringing something into it in the flying machines. One of the boys said it looked like ore of some sort. Maybe that thing they've built is a smelter or perhaps it's something more sinister. I have my own suspicions as to what they're up to but I hope I'm wrong. God knows we've got enough trouble without that."

"How many of the fifty would you say are in that area?"

"Thirty, thirty-five. The others patrol the city, picking up stray prisoners and taking them—dreadful thought—to the stockyards, where, I fear, they'll be putting the slaughter houses and meat-packing plants."

"We're not even slaves to them, are we?" Dylan said bitterly. "We're nothing but—"

"Vittles," H. said. "That's what Shawn said: 'Mr. H., them things ain't human. They don't want us for nothin' but a feed. We're just vittles to them.' So whatever your plan is . . ." He paused expectantly.

"It's a desperate one," Dylan said, "and it puts a terrible burden on Clarinda."

"But at least it's a plan," H. said. "None of the rest of us have even that much. Can you tell me about it?"

"It has two parts, either one of which could go wrong, and neither of which can be guaranteed successful. It depends on too many variables. Can you tell me if the dynamite factory near Ronderberry was destroyed?"

H. touched the pouch of bombs he wore. "That's where we get these. It's not only intact but so far the Martians haven't gone near it."

"Good! The first part of my plan is to get a motor truck, load it with dynamite, drive it through the back streets to the place where the Martians are concentrated and blow it up, killing as many of the monsters as I can."

"And yourself also, it would seem."

"I'll try to get away. But there is more to my plan than that, and this is the part I feel badly about. I'll have to use Clarinda's love for me to make her do something she's in mortal terror of doing—enter the Martians' minds, project something into them actually," Dylan said. "She is terrified of the cold, calculating nature of their minds because she feels they will somehow destroy her as a priestess, rob her of her power and leave her less than she is now. There is only one way I can force her to do it and I despise myself for being willing to resort to it, but with the fate of two worlds hanging in the balance . . ."

"The greater good for the greater number, as it were," H. said.

"Yes. If she knows that I am in mortal danger and there is only one way to save me, she'll do it," Dylan said unhappily. "I've got to put myself in such danger that she can only save me by projecting what I want her to into the minds of the Martians. It's a dirty, underhanded trick but . . ."

"I understand how you feel," H. said, "but what is it you want her to project and how do you think it will help?"

"During the fighting in the Silver Strand, when we destroyed one of the Martian battle machines, the occupant opened the hatch of its cupola and managed to scramble out only to be instantly killed by a shark."

"Good for the shark! I wish we could sic sharks on all of them!"

"We can't, but maybe we can make them believe we can," Dylan said. "I had an extraordinary experience once when I was on an expedition with my father in the southern hemisphere of Annwn. We had taken a diving bell along for deep-sea exploration of a particularly interesting lagoon in the Asmanian Archipelago. It was noted as the breeding place of the giant pink squid, and they came there from thousands of miles away to give birth to their multitudes of young. But also in the area were schools of great white sharks. One day while in the diving bell, I witnessed the sharks attacking and devouring the squid and their young by the thousands.

"It was a horrifying sight, and the sea for miles about was black with the ink and blood of the squid. The sight of that endless massacre made a profound impression on a youth of seventeen. I can still see those huge sharks with their monstrous mouths filled with razor-sharp teeth and the squid struggling to escape but being ripped to pieces. To this day that scene haunts my dreams from time to time. Now the Martians resemble those squid to a considerable degree, and my plan is for Clarinda to pick that vision from my mind and project it into the minds of the Martians. It might, at the very least, unnerve them."

H. nodded. "Yes, I can see that it might, but it would take a tremendous amount of mental power. Miss Clarinda has already weakened herself saving you from the wreck of the *Thunderbolt*."

"I know, but I've thought of a way we might augment her power," Dylan said, taking a piece of paper out of his sporran with an address on it. "Is there any means of communication out of the city?"

"Oddly enough, the wires to Amion have not been cut. I talked to your friend Noel there this morning. He was most anxious about you and Miss Clarinda."

"Does he have the *Vengeance* there?"

"Yes. She and three other naval airships escaped after the final battle with the Martian flying machines. She has been repaired and is ready when needed."

"Good. There is a person who must be brought to Avallon quickly to add to Clarinda's power," Dylan said. "I'll get messages off to Noel and his prospective passenger and then I'm on my way to find a large truck and load it with dynamite."

"I agree that this must be done," Mr. H. said, "but I'm afraid the chances of your scheme are even slimmer than you suggested. You're underestimating the danger of trying to move a load of dynamite through the streets with Martian patrols wandering around the city."

"It will be dark in about four hours," Dylan said. "If I can get the truck and load it by then, I'll drive through alleys and back streets to Greenfields, which will probably take me another three hours. Noel should be able to pick up the person we need and fly back to Avallon in about five hours. That should give Clarinda over an hour's time to work on the minds of the Martians before my dynamite goes off."

After looking in at the sleeping priestess and having a brief word with the wounded but recovering Churchward, Dylan left Trogtown with the eldest of Clarinda's brothers as a guide. They went through a tangle of old, unused, paved-over streets, ancient catacombs and sewers that the boy assured him would take him close to the dynamite factory in a northern suburb of Avallon.

Although it went against the grain for Mr. H. not to be in the middle of things, he and Dr. W. settled down to watch over Clarinda and wait for Dylan's plan to unfold. Four and a half hours later they were aroused from the dozes they had drifted into by the shouting and laughter of children and the booming of a deep male voice.

"Who's that?" Clarinda's eyes popped open and she raised herself on an elbow. "Whose voice was that I heard?"

"Clarinda MacTague, where are you, you lazy slug-a-bed?" The voice boomed again and a flashily dressed, balding, red-bearded giant of a man appeared in the doorway with five redheaded children clinging to his arms and one sitting on his back.

"Why, it's *himself*," Clarinda said, staring at her father in surprise.

"Of course 'tis himself," the big man said, striding over to stand by her bed, "and I've come to rouse you and turn you to for the savin' of mankind."

"No, no, I can't!" Clarinda said, cowering back against the pillow. Apparently there was no need for the father to tell the daughter any more than he had. She had picked the plan from his mind more quickly than it could be spoken.

"Get on with you, girl," her father said. "Why are you crouching here while the Empire, blast its Sassenach soul, stands in need of your powers, and the man you love goes to his death without a helpin' thought from you?"

Churchward hurried into the room, one arm in a sling and a bandage around his head, all excited. "Mr. H., Lady Philippa is gone! One of the younger boys said he saw her following Dylan."

"What?" Clarinda came up off the bed fast. "That wench has gone off to die with him in my place? I'll show her! I'll drag him back by his kilt and give him a piece of me mind!" She closed her eyes and gritted her teeth to work up a spell, but when her father's big hand connected with her bottom, the violet eyes flew open again.

"None of that, me girl," he said sternly. "There's a picture in your man's mind that should be scaring the daylights out of them Martians, and we're going to put it there in their minds just like he asked us to."

"But Dylan is goin' to get himself killed!" Clarinda wailed. "And in company with that woman!"

"Take me hand, girl," her father ordered, gesturing for everybody else to leave the room. "Take me hand and lead me mind to the mind of Dylan MacBride."

"But I ought to get Dylan out of there, I really ought." She was still protesting as she took her father's hand and together they began to search Dylan's memory for the image he wanted projected.

Dylan was sitting hunched over the steering wheel of a large steam truck, heading into a dark alley off Clas Myrddn Way when there was a sound behind him. He turned his head to see Lady Philippa crawling out from under the canvas that covered the boxes of dynamite loaded in the back.

"What the devil are you doing here?" he demanded when the girl had slid down into the seat beside him.

"I decided to go with you. If you're going to die because of something I helped bring about, then I'm going to die also."

"Don't be a fool," Dylan said. "Alone I might have a chance, with you along, I have none. I even sent the boy back."

"Let me go instead. My life doesn't matter, and at least I will have tried to make amends."

"You sound like the reformed villainess in a bad novel," he said. "I know what I'm doing. My plans are carefully made and they don't include dragging any hysterical woman along with me."

"I am not hysterical," she said. "Do I sound hysterical?"

"No, but . . ." It occurred to Dylan that there wasn't much he could do about her being here. He couldn't leave her alone in the dark streets knowing she would almost certainly be set upon by a patrolling Martian. "I suppose you'll have to come with me. I haven't got time to take you back."

"At least I'll feel that I've done something," she said.

"You have," he said gruffly. "You've made it harder for me to succeed." He looked at his watch. There was only an hour left of the schedule he had set, forty-five minutes to reach the area of the mysterious factory the Martians had set up and light the fuses on the bombs, and fifteen minutes to get into one of the sewers and as far from the scene as possible. In the meantime, he had to hope that Clarinda and the Great MacTague were addling the Martians' minds with the vision he had felt them pick out of his.

They were about a block from their destination when they ran into trouble. For some time they had seen bright blue lights ahead of them and an occasional outline of a Martian handling machine busily at work. Nearby, seemingly in conference about something, were thirty or thirty-five of the battle machines, looming like giants over the wreckage of the airship hangars. A continual cacophony of hooting sounds rose over the noise of the clanking, whirring machinery.

"They're agitated about something," Lady Philippa said.

"I don't suppose you can pick anything out of their minds?"

"Well, I don't have Clarinda's power but I can get a little. They're trying to confer about what they're building in that factory. I get the word pitchblende and . . . uranium and some kind of weapon they are creating in case they need it. They're impressed with the human race's powers of resistance but they are certain this new weapon will crush mankind utterly. But that isn't what they're agitated about. It's something else."

"I hope it's the sight of giant sharks devouring tiny and some not so tiny Martians," Dylan said, and turned at a sudden hooting near at hand. There was a Martian behind them, striding after them and hooting the alarm to his fellows.

"We've got to go for it now," Dylan said as another Martian and then a third and fourth appeared, striding over the wrecks of houses and swinging their heat-rays into position to fire. He pressed his foot down on the drive lever of the truck and steered straight for the factory.

"I don't think we're going to make it. We're too far away from the main body of them to harm them with the dynamite."

"What about the factory itself?" Philippa asked. "Can we destroy it? It has a feeling of terrible menace about it."

The Martians were almost on them now, apparently holding their fire in order to take them alive. Dylan drew his revolver as the lorry skidded to a stop beside the metallic wall of the Martian building. It was as close as they were going to get and Dylan knew it. There wasn't time to light the fuses. He would have to take a more direct method of setting off the explosive. A hooting Martian was about a dozen feet from them now, its tentacles reaching out.

"I'm sorry, Philippa," he said, aiming his pistol at the dynamite and pulling the trigger.

"*Dylan! Dylan!*" a woman's voice screamed and then the world dissolved in sound and light before total darkness descended.

"So there you are, me sleepin' beauty," a booming voice said. "Is it comin' 'round now that you're doin'?"

Dylan opened his eyes to stare up at a giant red-bearded man in a checkered suit and derby who was bending over him.

"Well, you slept through most of it, you know," the Great MacTague said.

"Slept through most of what?" Dylan asked.

"Most of the final battle of the Second War of the Worlds," MacTague said, "and a frightful noisy thing it was."

"You mean . . ." Suddenly it all came back to Dylan. "I remember aiming my revolver at the dynamite and—My God, I ought to be dead!"

"And so you would be if that sweet lass of mine hadn't taken her mind off tormentin' the Martians with sharks long enough to grab you and the beautiful black-haired lady out of the midst of the greatest explosion the world has ever seen."

"The greatest explosion? You mean the dynamite?"

"He means the dynamite plus the thing the Martians were building," Mr. H. said. "And that, I do believe, was an atomic bomb of the sort Mr. Wells described in his scientific romance, *The World Set Free*. Fancy the Martians being able to build one, to crack the very atom for destructive power."

"Thanks be to Keridwen that they never got to use it," MacTague said.

"And thanks be to Dylan that his dynamite set it off in the midst of them that built it before they could use it against us," Clarinda's voice said from directly over his head and Dylan realized he was lying in her lap.

"Clarinda, darling, I thought I'd never see you again when I pulled the trigger of that revolver."

"Sure now, and you wouldn't be thinkin' I'd be lettin' you die in the company of that Philippa wench, would you? Why, I'd as soon let you marry her."

Dylan laughed and kissed her hand, and the Great MacTague cleared his throat noisily. "There's something I been meanin' to ask you, me bye."

"What's that?" Dylan asked.

"I want to know if you be thinkin' of marryin' me daughter and makin' a proper wife of her, or do you have other ideas in mind?"

Dylan stared at the huge man, impressed by his size and the hamlike fists. "Of course I'm going to marry her," he said. "Just as soon as the Martians are defeated."

"Then that would likely be today," the MacTague said. "That dynamite set off that atomic bomb of theirs, diggin' a hole big enough to put half the city in and wipin' out all but a half dozen or so of them things. Old General Horwitz and his army and airships are huntin' down the rest, and with their minds befuddled by the terrible vision of themselves being eaten by monsters, they'll not be puttin' up much of a resistance."

"In that case," Dylan said, "I guess we better name the day."

A week later, Mr. and Mrs. Dylan MacBride and a proud new father-in-law saw Mr. H. and Dr. W. off in the *Vengeance*. Noel had obtained permission to fly them to Caer Pendryvan where the Shimmering Gates connected Annwn to her twin planet, Earth.

Lady Philippa was going back to England with them, there to face charges of high treason and disturbing the peace.

She kissed Dylan lightly and smiled at Clarinda. "Be good to him, my dear. He's worth it."

"I will be," Clarinda said with an answering smile that was just a little too sweet. "And I hope they won't be too hard on you in the courts."

Watching her, Dylan was sure she was secretly hoping for an English hanging jury.

When the newlyweds, along with the bride's father and brothers and sisters, were attending the reception Lady Alice gave in their honor, Dylan remarked a little sadly that they would probably never see Philippa again.

"Don't be too sure," Clarinda said, violet eyes snapping. "She's one of them brainy women and that kind is always a year's worth of trouble in a day!"

Presenting JOHN NORMAN in DAW editions . . .

☐ **TRIBESMEN OF GOR.** The tenth novel of Tarl Cabot takes him face to face with the Others' most dangerous plot—in the vast Tahari desert with its warring tribes, its bandit queen, and its treachery. (#UW1223—$1.50)

☐ **HUNTERS OF GOR.** The saga of Tarl Cabot on Earth's orbital counterpart reaches a climax as Tarl seeks his lost Talena among the outlaws and panther women of the wilderness. (#UW1102—$1.50)

☐ **MARAUDERS OF GOR.** The ninth novel of Tarl Cabot's adventures takes him to the northland of transplanted Vikings and into direct confrontation with the enemies of two worlds. (#UW1160—$1.50)

☐ **TIME SLAVE.** The creator of Gor brings back the days of the caveman in a vivid new novel of time travel and human destiny. (#UW1204—$1.50)

☐ **IMAGINATIVE SEX.** A study of the sexuality of male and female which leads to a new revelation of sensual liberation. Fifty-three imaginative situations are outlined, some of which are science-fictional in nature.
(#UJ1146—$1.95)

DAW BOOKS are represented by the publishers of Signet and Mentor Books, THE NEW AMERICAN LIBRARY, INC.